Who Killed th

His wife said it was someone who feared him as head of the Parents League....

His priest told the police not to listen to her....

His foremost adversary had million-dollar motives and no alibi....

And John Putnam Thatcher, whether he liked it or not, was being drawn into a baffling case of high tension, high finance and highly unorthodox passion.

Books by Emma Lathen

Ashes to Ashes
Death Shall Overcome
Double Double Oil and Trouble
The Longer the Thread
Murder Without Icing
Pick Up Sticks
A Place for Murder

Published by POCKET BOOKS

EMMA LATHEN

ASHES TO ASHES

PUBLISHED BY POCKET BOOKS NEW YORK

Distributed in Canada by PaperJacks Ltd., a Licensee
of the trademarks of Simon & Schuster, a division of
Gulf + Western Corporation.

POCKET BOOKS, a Simon & Schuster division of
GULF & WESTERN CORPORATION
1230 Avenue of the Americas, New York, N.Y. 10020
In Canada distributed by PaperJacks Ltd.,
330 Steelcase Road, Markham, Ontario.

CONTENTS

ASHES TO ASHES

1

THE PLACE OF GREAT MEN

Wall Street is the largest and most efficient market the world has ever known. The harried messengers, the peremptory teletypes, the untold millions of abstracts, prospectuses, briefs, reports, invoices, certificates and receipts are only means. The end is a smooth and orderly transaction, even when the buyer is in Macao, the seller in Ankara, and the copper still below ground in Zambia.

But even dynamic young portfolio managers admit that Wall Street knows unscheduled departures from perfection. Fortunately, these can be explained. Scrambled margin accounts, double billing and visionary profit estimates are invariably caused by computer error; five-week delays in stock transfers, disappearing warrants, and garbled information are attributable to human frailty. Only salad oil and certain accounting methods raise the ugly question of original sin.

This is the canon of the street. John Putnam Thatcher, senior vice president of the Sloan Guaranty Trust, was willing to accept it as far as it went. You get along by going along in places other than Washington. And few men had gotten further along in this demanding world than Thatcher. The Sloan was a mighty institution, with resources rivaled only by the great superpowers.

It was not the perch from which to view Wall Street with detachment. Especially when the Dow Jones average has just dropped thirty points in one week.

It was John Thatcher's private theory that during such major downward shifts, the financial community as a whole went slightly and temporarily insane. Orders went undischarged. Syndicates fell apart. Drinking men went on the wagon and abstainers swilled four martinis before lunch.

Whenever four hundred thousand shares of any blue chip had to be sold in the third market, virtually all of Thatcher's colleagues developed alarming aberrations.

It was Thatcher's custom during such trying intervals to seek out the exceptions. In practice, he reflected as he fought his way up William Street against a bitter cutting wind and a tide of office-bent secretaries, this meant that market crises often found him lunching with Stanton Carruthers. Carruthers was a trust and estate lawyer. Trusts (and estates) as viewed from Carruthers & Carruthers were momentous matters, measured by a stately concept of time—namely, the generation. Frequently to the fourth and fifth. Men who think in terms of generations are not given to fits and starts.

Whether the profession made the man, or the man found the profession, Stanton Carruthers, whom Thatcher found awaiting him at The Coachman, was reassuringly free from the tics afflicting everybody else these days. A tall man with meticulous manners, he was a compendium of sober virtues. He did not ask for the inside story on why the American Exchange had suspended trading in Roote Industries, or even about the Tallahassee Fund's bizarre selling patterns.

"Good to see you, John," he said, unfolding a napkin and scanning the menu with perfunctory interest.

Thatcher replied appropriately.

After the ritual of ordering, Stanton Carruthers continued in kind.

"I understand you're in charge these days," he said.

"Yes indeed," said Thatcher, who was currently acting president of the Sloan Guaranty Trust.

"Where's George?" Carruthers inquired.

How wise he had been to choose Carruthers, Thatcher congratulated himself. Almost no one on the financial side of the street could have refrained from witticism at this juncture. Not with the average still sliding toward ten-year lows. For Thatcher became acting president of the bank only in the absence of his two superiors—Bradford Withers, president, and George C. Lancer, chairman of the board. Withers was a notorious peripatetic. He was at the moment, for reasons not clear to Thatcher, in Ulan Bator. George, thank God, was a dedicated banker with a high sense of duty. Trust Stanton Carruthers to make things easy.

"George," Thatcher was able to reply, "is in Washington, testifying before Wright Patman."

Carruthers resisted even this temptation.

Of course, there were those who claimed that witticism on any subject did not tempt Carruthers. Certainly, the ensuing conversation could not be described as scintillating. Nevertheless, Thatcher found it quite satisfactory. There are times, after all, when absolute predictability has its charms.

As a man and as a banker, John Putnam Thatcher should have remembered that there is no such thing as absolute predictability.

Refreshed, Thatcher returned to his office, ready to resume battle. He was prepared for anguished cries from each and every one of his subordinates. He was prepared for rapid deterioration in the Investment Division. He was even prepared for apocalyptic visions in Commercial Loan.

He was not prepared for a subpoena on his desk.

"*Francis P. Omara vs. Joseph, Cardinal Devlin,*" he read aloud. "What the devil . . . ?"

Miss Corsa, his secretary, who was a faithful daughter of her church, looked at him disapprovingly.

Thatcher felt moved to defend himself. "I have no idea what this is about, Miss Corsa. Do we have any memos on the subject?"

"I do not believe so," she replied coldly. It should not have been necessary to remind him that any memos on the subject of lawsuits brought against His Eminence, the Roman Catholic Archbishop of New York, were not likely to have escaped her attention. Nevertheless, Miss Corsa made a rapid review of the items that George C. Lancer had referred to Mr. Thatcher's attention.

"No, Mr. Thatcher," she announced after a few moments. "Shall I check around?"

"Please do," said Thatcher politely.

Naturally, he could not foresee where this was going to lead. He was, however, given a reasonable foretaste by his incomparably disinterested secretary.

Miss Corsa returned with information and a series of ap-

pointments superseding his existing appointments. Since Miss
Corsa had a rigid sense of priorities, Thatcher saw that she,
at least, regarded *Francis P. Omara vs. Joseph, Cardinal
Devlin* as worthier of attention than the imminent collapse of
the stock market.

"The Sloan," she announced as preliminary to her subsequent report, "is financing the purchase of a parochial grade
school. St. Bernadette's—in Flensburg. Mr. Llewellyn from
Real Estate is on his way up. The Law Department will brief
you at three. Public Relations will call when they have
finished getting background material . . ."

Predictably, neither Real Estate nor Law could match Miss
Corsa's conciseness. Nevertheless, by ruthlessly damming a
flood of technical information concerning assessed valuations
and zoning ordinances, Thatcher managed to obtain some
facts. The Sloan was indeed involved in the purchase of St.
Bernadette's Parochial School.

This was not the way that the Real Estate Department
liked to think of the transaction.

The Archdiocese of New York proposed to sell a parcel of
land in Queens to the Unger Realty Corporation, an old and
valued Sloan client. This land, encompassing ninety thousand
square feet, was intended by Unger Realty as the site for a
high-rise apartment complex. The Sloan was providing mortgage money, to the tune of four million dollars. Sloan experts,
from architects to appraisers, had examined everything with
a fine-toothed comb.

". . . first-rate location, near the subway," said Llewellyn
with dusty enthusiasm. "The neighborhood is not what it
once was, so costs won't be exorbitant. And there will be a
substantial increase in value when Unger is finished. It's a
sweet proposition."

"Yes indeed," said Thatcher. "But why does it involve us
in a lawsuit, Llewellyn? For that matter, what is this lawsuit
about?"

In many ways, Llewellyn was a limited man. "It is not a
matter of title," he said stiffly.

Thatcher had never doubted this. There was one thing to
be said about Sloan mortgages: their purity of title was
virginal.

"Parents!" said Stetson from the Law Department. "There's a parents group out there, protesting the closing of the school. I just called Ericson. He's filed for an injunction to stop the sale of the land. I don't know anything about religious law, but he's attacking the theory that a parish school belongs to the Archbishop. We're being summoned as witnesses."

"Ericson?" Thatcher inquired.

Willard Ericson was representing the Parents League, Stetson explained. He then added: "Ericson's one of Stan Carruthers' partners."

"Hmm," said Thatcher.

"That's the only thing that makes me think there may be something in this," said Stetson airily, ignoring Llewellyn's tendency to bristle. "This kind of nuisance suit is usually some bunch of nuts, with an ambitious lawyer trying to make a name for himself. But God only knows why Ericson's doing it."

Miss Corsa took an altogether graver view. No sooner had Thatcher's office been cleared, than she was back.

"The public relations people have not found anything yet," she said.

"You surprise me," Thatcher told her.

But Miss Corsa was not deflected. "Miss Bellotti," she told her employer, "who works in Statistical Typing, comes from Flensburg."

"Ah ha!" said Thatcher. It was nice to know that the Sloan's information sources were not limited to its overpaid upper echelons. "And what does Miss Bellotti say?"

He heard Miss Corsa's rendition of the Bellotti version. Miss Bellotti, a newcomer to the Sloan, had not felt equal to reporting directly. She was, he gathered, a giddy young thing. Filtering giddiness through Miss Corsa was always excellent procedure.

Flensburg, in the borough of Queens, was thirty-five minutes by subway from midtown Manhattan, a neighborhood not so homogeneous as it had once been, but still a community of modest comfort. For generations, St. Bernadette's Church and St. Bernadette's School had contributed to that sense of community.

"Gee," Miss Bellotti had said, "I went there myself!"

"I see," said Thatcher.

Four months ago, church authorities had announced that rising costs and the familiar financial squeeze would force closing of the school by the end of the school year. There was unhappiness throughout the parish with this decision. But unhappiness turned to anger one week later. The Archdiocese had then announced that Unger Realty planned to buy St. Bernadette's, demolish its buildings and construct a twenty-story apartment house.

"That," Miss Bellotti had said gleefully, "really got everybody going!"

Earlier protests hardened. An organization instantly formed. Night after night there were meetings of parents. People distributed handouts at the subway entrance during rush hour.

Since there were no colleges or universities in the Flensburg area, this was the first organized dissent the community had witnessed. It was, or so Miss Bellotti said, really kind of exciting.

"Thank you very much, Miss Corsa," said Thatcher when she had finished.

Miss Corsa said demurely that he was welcome. And also, Mr. Unger was on the line.

Thatcher watched her depart with uplifted eyebrow. He did not resent being stage-managed on occasion, but he was by no means sure that this was the occasion. A nuisance suit against the Roman Catholic Church was not likely to bring that august institution to its knees. However, Miss Corsa had placed Mr. Unger on his line. It behooved him to back her up.

"Dad is in Jamaica," said the voice on the phone. "I'm handling the St. Bernadette's sale."

Thatcher had met Dad. Unger senior, an aggressive real estate entrepreneur, had built a small firm into one of New York's largest. His methods had earned him a reputation as a rough diamond; if he had been less successful, the description would have been different. The son, Thatcher recalled, was not a rough diamond.

"Yes, we had heard that there might be some trouble,"

Dick Unger went on. "But we didn't expect to get a sub-poena!"

Thatcher agreed that it was unusual.

Dick Unger sounded bemused. "You know, I've talked to Frank Omara myself. He's the chairman of this bunch of parents. You'd think that he'd understand the situation more than some of the others. He's an undertaker."

"A profitable occupation," Thatcher commented.

"That's right," Unger said. "He should see that the parish literally can't afford to keep the school running. And if they're not going to operate a school, they'd be fools to turn down a good offer for the property. It isn't as if we were planning to put up a factory. If anything, property values are going to go up once we've built."

Thatcher agreed that this was simple logic and inquired where Francis Omara failed to follow.

He elicited a muffled groan. "I can't really say," said Dick Unger, baffled. "He starts talking about Catholic education—and he loses me!"

Thatcher did not remind the young man that these were deep waters. Instead, he asked about Unger Realty's immediate position.

"We're still counting on the sale going through," said Unger with some of his father's bluntness. "By the time we've built, well, we're hoping that all this will be a thing of the past. I don't think a suit against the Cardinal is going to hold us up for long, do you?"

"Not unless they've got something up their sleeves," said Thatcher.

He was now prepared to put St. Bernadette's from his mind and concentrate on more germane matters. But Miss Corsa was not through with him yet.

"Mr. Ericson," she announced, "will meet you at The Coachman for lunch tomorrow."

She was not shaken by Thatcher's silent reproof.

"Miss Corsa," he said solemnly, "if anybody in this bank should require my attention on any subject other than a parochial school, will you be good enough to refer them to Trinkam?"

Without blinking, Miss Corsa assured him this would be done.

It left him with an uneasy feeling that Miss Corsa saw more than he did.

2

REMOVE NOT THE OLD LANDMARK

For the second day in a row, Thatcher found himself lunching at The Coachman with a lawyer. He felt that this might be interpreted as overdoing. Regrettably, it was not a commendable sense of duty that steered his thoughts along these lines. It was the impact of Willard Ericson.

Within minutes of meeting the man, Thatcher had taken his measure. He was a fanatic. In appearance, he was a conservative Wall Street lawyer. But something about his intent gaze put Thatcher on his guard.

Lunch at The Coachman was already repetitive. He could do without religious mania.

By the time they had progressed to roast beef, Ericson had disabused Thatcher of his error. His fervor, it became clear, was reserved for the purely legal implications of the sale of St. Bernadette's School.

". . . Religious Corporation Act," he said, happily spearing a potato.

"Interesting," said Thatcher. In point of fact, the Religious Corporation Act is almost totally devoid of interest. "Tell me," he said hastily, before Ericson could get under way again, "does this lawsuit have any real possibility of success? After all, as I understand it, the property does in fact belong to the Archdiocese."

"Ah ha!" Ericson pounced loudly enough to turn heads at nearby tables. "That is precisely the point that bears inspection. Very careful inspection. Perhaps you recall the case of the Russian Orthodox Cathedral in Buffalo?"

He rattled on despite Thatcher's firm denials. Ericson was prepared to use any comment as launching pad for a lecture on esoteric points of law in regard to religious institutions. It occurred to Thatcher that combining this legal virtuosity with Miss Bellotti's excitement might spell trouble.

And a four-million-dollar mortgage is a four-million-dollar mortgage.

"What was that?" Ericson barked. The only way to get a word in was to bulldoze through. Thatcher repeated his question.

"Yes indeed," said Willard Ericson keenly. "We have very good reason to believe that we can delay this sale long enough for our purposes."

What, Thatcher inquired, were those purposes?

"To prevent the sale to Unger," Ericson said. "With a long enough delay, Unger will certainly have to look elsewhere. That will put an entirely different complexion on the whole St. Bernadette's situation. I think there is a strong possibility that the courts will . . ."

To do the man justice, he was totally without malice as he enthusiastically outlined schemes to thwart the Roman Catholic Church, Unger Realty and the Sloan Guaranty Trust.

"And your . . . er . . . clients?" Thatcher interpolated. "Is a delay going to be enough to satisfy them?"

He should have known better. Ericson might be a legal philosopher-king, but he was not the man to provide useful insights into the parish of St. Bernadette's or its up-in-arms parents.

"Oh, I think so," he said vaguely. "One thing I'll say for them. They're a very determined lot."

"Splendid," said Thatcher heartily. He was always willing to enlarge his experience. But it was a shame he was stuck with Ericson on Wall Street.

The action, or so Ericson led him to believe, was elsewhere. In Flensburg.

In Flensburg, there was no ambiguity about what the St. Bernadette's Parents League thought. At that very moment one of its members, Mrs. Patricia Ianello, was earnestly outlining her position. She sat behind a battered wooden desk in a store-front office.

"No, Sheila," she was saying with rapidly rising exasperation. "This has nothing to do with married priests. Honestly! Why don't you just listen to what I'm saying?"

"And then there are all these changes in the Mass." Her companion preferred complaining to listening. "I liked the Mass the way it was. I don't see why people have to change everything around."

"But we don't want to change anything!" Pat almost howled. She glared across the desk. Sheila Macdonald had been in her class at St. Bernadette's. Now they both had children in the first grade. In the intervening twenty years, she had never before felt any desire to choke Sheila.

"Look, Sheila, it's really very simple," she said slowly. "You and I went to St. Bernadette's, didn't we?"

Sheila frowned, examined the question from every angle, and then nodded reluctantly.

"And now we want Betty and Kevin to go to St. Bernadette's, don't we?"

Again that same wary agreement.

"And so," Pat concluded triumphantly, "we don't want any changes. We want things to stay unchanged. And you are on the same side as the Parents League!"

Sheila looked startled but not downright hostile.

"So there's no reason why you shouldn't sign our petition." Pat produced a long sheet of paper with two small paragraphs at the top and hundreds of signature spaces beneath. At the same time she extended a pen suggestively.

Sheila closed her hands into defensive fists and said that Dan didn't hold with her signing things. Besides she didn't want to go against the Church.

"This isn't going against the . . ." Pat began before braking to a sudden halt. She then took a deep breath and produced a smile which would not have deceived a chance passerby. "Maybe you should take one of our pamphlets home for Dan to read. I'm sure he'll agree with us, once he realizes Kevin may not be able to go to St. Bernadette's."

The mimeographed brochure was accepted, but Sheila Macdonald lingered long enough in the doorway to say dubiously that Dan wasn't a great one for reading. Then she exchanged greetings with the woman entering and was gone.

"Well, Pat, how did it go?" asked the newcomer.

Pat's answer was to arch back over her chair in a huge bone-stretching yawn. Then, smacking her diaphragm sharply, she collapsed.

"Ouf!" she announced.

With her slight, boyish body and scrubbed, freckled face, Pat Ianello scarcely looked old enough to qualify for a parents organization. She ran a hand through her straight light-brown hair before replying thoughtfully:

"Either I'm no good at explaining things or the people in this parish are a lot dumber than I ever realized."

Mary Foster was amused.

"You feel that way now, Pat, because it's our first try at organizing something. You'll get used to it."

"I'm not sure I want to," Pat said frankly.

"Oh, come on," was the answer. "It's no crime to admit that people in groups are stupider than people taken one by one."

"Is that what politics teaches you?"

"Politics!" Mary Foster snorted from the sink where she was filling a coffeepot. "It takes more than losing one race for Borough Council to make me a politician."

Pat grinned. She was not taken in by this mock modesty. Mary Foster was a big buxom woman overflowing with vitality. At forty-two she was just beginning to hit her stride.

"Never mind. I'll bet you win the next time."

"I wouldn't mind doing it from here. This was my campaign headquarters, you know." Mary looked around the improvised office. "So far, it's been the home of nothing but lost hopes."

Pat straightened up. "What do you mean, lost hopes?" she asked alertly. "Don't you think we'll save St. Bernadette's? You remember what Mr. Ericson said?"

"Don't jump down my throat! We won't save it forever, that's all I meant. Even with Ericson on our side. We're fighting a holding action. Two or three years is all we can hope for. And to tell the truth, with my youngest boy in fifth grade, that's all I need."

"Two or three years." Pat was reflective. "Of course, Betty is just in the first grade and Eddie hasn't even started, but Sal thinks he'll get a new store in a couple of years and then we'd probably have to move away. Sal says there's no point in thinking farther ahead."

Like everyone who dealt with Pat, Mary Foster was used to hearing the views of Salvatore Ianello quoted.

"Speaking of Sal," she said, "you didn't forget to tell him about the rally next week?"

"No, I didn't forget. Sal says we can have the urn and ten pounds of coffee."

"It comes in handy, having an A&P manager in the Parents League."

"Yes," said Pat absently. She was staring fixedly out the front window. "This is really a very convenient location. You can see right across the street."

Mary swiveled to follow her glance. Spread before them were the visible symbols of the Roman Catholic presence in Flensburg—the church itself, flanked by the rectory and the parochial school and, beyond the playground, the small convent for the teaching nuns.

A view both of them had seen countless times, Mary reminded herself. Why call attention to it now?

"Do you mean you can see your enemy?" she asked uneasily. "But you *like* St. Bernadette's."

Pat shook her shoulders as if to break a spell. Then her clear laughter floated out.

"Of course that's not it! I mean you can see when school lets out. Which it's doing now. Betty has to be picked up. Goodbye, it's time I went back to work."

Of course, most of the St. Bernadette's Parents League had been working all day. In fact Bob Horvath had already finished his seven-to-three shift as a truck driver. He was returning home when he had the bad luck to meet one of his neighbors at the elevator.

"Hello, Phil," he said unenthusiastically.

Phil Kavanaugh, a dried-up little bantam, was pugnacious. "I saw your poster. For a rally about St. Bernadette's."

"That's right."

"You ought to be ashamed of yourselves. A lot of trouble-makers, egging each other on. Father James thinks so, too."

"Have you read our pamphlet?"

"I wouldn't be caught reading that muck."

"That's what I thought."

Kavanaugh shifted his attack. "Is it true that you're taking His Eminence to court?"

"You've got it in one."

"And who are you to be setting yourselves above the Cardinal? Has the Pope suddenly made you an archbishop?"

Horvath quelled the impulse to take Kavanaugh by the collar and chuck him down the elevator shaft. Instead he pressed the elevator button for the third time.

"Lay off, Phil," he said wearily. "Nobody cares what you think."

But whether he cared or not, Bob Horvath had the benefit of his neighbor's opinions all the way up to the fourth floor.

"That Kavanaugh is beginning to get to me, Ruthie," he exploded to his wife. "Who the hell does he think he is, trying to tell me what school to send my kids to? A guy that's always been too cheap to get married himself!"

Ruthie picked up his windbreaker from the floor. "Now, honey," she soothed. "Phil's not so bad."

Horvath scowled at her. He was a firm believer that sweetness and charity were desirable characteristics in women but, honest to God, sometimes Ruthie carried things too far.

"He told me himself," Ruthie persevered, "that he stayed single for his mother's sake."

Bob Horvath's braying laugh could have been heard two floors away. (It quite frequently was and had occasioned many tenant complaints.)

"Oh yeah? And what about the time he threw the can of tomato juice at her?" He paused dramatically. "The jumbo size!"

Francis Omara did not work to a strict schedule. As befitted one of the owners of Flensburg's largest funeral home, he managed plenty of time off for vacations, golf and family outings. At the moment, however, distinguished and reassuring in a dark striped suit, he was leaving a home where he had outlined funeral arrangements. By his side was the newest curate in the parish.

"Well, that's that," Omara said briskly. "Going my way, Father?"

Omara was not being professionally heartless. Death had just come to a ninety-three-year-old great-grandmother. A display of shocked grief would have been out of place. But Father James, fresh from the seminary, found the right manner eluding him.

"The family is bearing up very well," he said in a voice that sounded priggish even to his own ears.

Omara grinned. "Most people are pretty realistic," he said, stepping out buoyantly. "My car is two blocks up."

"So is mine." The younger man was having difficulty keeping pace. Moreover he regretted the appearance of that grin. He wanted to speak seriously and he had hoped that the background of death would create the atmosphere he might have trouble achieving himself.

Gathering his courage, he went on: "I know that you're associated with this Parents League, Mr. Omara. I think I should tell you that I cannot approve of your actions."

Francis Omara was twenty years older than the curate and had spent his whole life in Flensburg. The rebuke of a newly arrived priest did not overwhelm him. On the contrary, there was some danger that his amusement might be apparent. He reminded himself of the courtesies due the cloth. Cocking a quizzical eyebrow, he said soberly, "I'm sorry to hear you say that, Father. I hope you believe that we're only trying to do the right thing."

Like most of his contemporaries, Father James was skeptical of the moral commitment of anyone over thirty.

"That's just what I can't believe," he burst out. "It's not as if I don't approve of lay participation in church affairs. If this were a matter of conscience, I'd be the first to sympathize. But all this talk about wanting a Catholic education, when you know that you're just trying to avoid sending your children to school with blacks. . . . It's the hypocrisy of it that sickens me."

Morticians necessarily learn to deal with emotional outbursts. Omara's geniality was unimpaired.

"Come now, Father. We're not all such evil sinners," he said easily. "I'm a prosperous man myself. I could afford to sidestep the public school, you know. But I want my children to go to St. Bernadette's. You're right that it's not just a matter of Catholic education. It's a matter of a community parish too."

Father James had not planned their talk this way. He had seen himself as magisterially reproving. The undertaker, naturally, would have lost his normal air of self-sufficient good cheer. He would have been penitent, brought to see the duplicity of his own motives. Perhaps not immediately. Initially he might have blustered, been defensive, forgotten the respect due a priest. The last thing he was supposed to be was calmly indulgent to the enthusiasms of his curate. Father James had a dim suspicion that, to Francis Omara, he was an inexperienced boy. And that Omara could not bring himself to be harsh to a boy.

"That is not true of most of the members of the League," he rejoined, trying to force the issue.

"I can only speak for my own motives." If anything Omara's tone was now even kindlier. He did, however, change the subject. "I am sorry that Father Doyle isn't able to be up and about."

"Father Doyle is in bed with the flu," said Father James stiffly. Was he being reminded that the parish priest was the man to censure his parishioners?

Francis Omara paused by his car. His blue eyes were very bright against his deep tan. They were twinkling as he said, "Father Doyle always times his bouts of the flu very well. They almost always come when he wants to avoid taking a public stand on some issue. He's learned a lot of wisdom in his years, Father Doyle has."

When his black Cadillac pulled away from the curb, Father James stood for some time looking after it.

"What can you do with people like that?" he asked himself for the hundredth time.

"We must remember that these people are undoubtedly very sincere," Monsignor Miles said firmly. One look at his two companions had been enough to convince him that it would be well to make this point.

They were sitting in the archdiocesan office on Madison Avenue, planning immediate tactics. The long-term strategy had been laid down by His Eminence before departure for Rome.

"Sincere?" gasped Henry Stonor, the archdiocesan public relations man. "They have filed a suit against the archdiocese!" He was a layman, but his piety was second to no one's.

It was left to a cleric to voice a more sophisticated denunciation.

"They are challenging the right of the Archbishop to dispose of church property. Think what that could lead to!"

For a moment rapt silence prevailed. Monsignor Miles was bemused by the vision of rampant laymen auctioning off St. Patrick's.

Or St. Peter's?

He roused himself. "Naturally I agree they are misguided," he said sharply. "But I would prefer to approach them more in sorrow than in anger. Please bear in mind that we officially regard the members of the St. Bernadette's Parents League as erring children—not apostates!"

His associates were obviously not persuaded. They were, he was pleased to see, ready to set the parish of St. Bernadette's a good example in the matter of obedience to spiritual superiors.

Monsignor Miles relaxed his tone. "As Father Livingston has said, think where this could lead. This is exactly the problem we have to address ourselves to. If a court action really takes place, it will become a magnet for every malcontent in the archdiocese. His Eminence has directed me to make every possible effort to reason with the Parents League."

His audience stirred restively but remained silent.

"I think I should meet with them. If possible, I would like to have representatives of the buyer, Unger Realty, present also. Do we have any idea of their current position?"

"Yes, Monsignor." Henry Stonor leaned forward, an anxious frown on his face. "Mr. Unger himself called after being served with a subpoena. He said he was unhappy about the publicity."

"He is not the only one," Monsignor Miles replied crisply.

The dissatisfaction of Father Livingston could no longer be contained.

"It's not as if His Eminence hadn't explained the situation fully to this Parents League. We gave them all the facts and figures. They can see for themselves that, with increased school populations and fewer teaching nuns, it is no longer possible to finance the school. I sometimes think these parents cannot be reached by the voice of reason."

Monsignor Miles's lean, lined face suddenly creased into a smile. "Then, dreadful as it must seem, we may have to fall back on the voice of faith."

3

GRIEVOUS WORDS

"There's going to be a meeting of the principals in this St. Bernadette's business tomorrow night," Dick Unger reported by phone. "Monsignor Miles is making a last-minute bid to settle out of court. He's suggested that we might like to come along."

"Oh, yes?" said Thatcher neutrally, braced to resist any suggestion that he personally represent the Sloan. Real Estate had perpetrated this mess. Let Real Estate spend its evenings in Flensburg. "Where is the meeting being held?"

Unger sounded morose. "That seems to be something of a problem. They're having trouble reaching an agreement."

"Unless they decide on a meeting place, there can scarcely be a meeting," Thatcher pointed out. Simple logic always seemed to be at a premium during these complex negotiations.

"I think they finally understand that," Unger said hastily. "But you see, it started with Monsignor Miles's suggesting that they all meet here in town, at the archdiocesan office. The parents wouldn't go along with that—they said it was an attempt to overawe them with spiritual authority. So, they said, what about the store where they have their headquarters? But Stonor—he's Miles's publicity man—is afraid that would imply the Church recognizes this Parents League as a legitimate organization. He says this is a private lawsuit by Francis Omara. They kicked around the notion of meeting in a lawyer's office, but everybody said that would make it look too adversarial for a meeting of co-religionists."

"Is anybody claiming that this meeting is not adversarial?" Thatcher inquired.

Dick Unger replied that it was hard to tell. He then pressed on to ask if Thatcher were willing to come.

Somewhat to his own surprise, Thatcher found that he could not resist the opportunity.

Not that Thatcher journeyed to Flensburg the next evening with high hopes. He knew that professional diplomats and union negotiators can husband their energy during preliminaries such as settling location, agenda and order of precedence. But amateurs, in his opinion, all too often exhausted themselves on these trivia—only to reach the bargaining table with additional grievances and very short fuses indeed.

The meeting did not begin auspiciously.

"This is Mr. Omara who has filed the suit," ran the introduction, "and by his side are some of his fellow-parents—Mrs. Foster, Mr. Horvath and Mr. and Mrs. Ianello."

Willard Ericson folded his hands and looked benignly across the table. "Collectively the group is usually referred to as the Action Committee of the St. Bernadette's Parents League," he informed the surrounding air.

"So I understand," Father James replied. His tone convinced Thatcher, at least, that he would rather go to the stake than make any such reference.

Monsignor Miles intervened. "Perhaps we could continue

with the introductions," he said briskly. "Mr. Omara, I believe that you have already met Mr. Unger, the purchaser of the property. And this is Mr. Thatcher, representing the Sloan Guaranty Trust."

Civil nods had been substituted for hearty handshakes. This, Thatcher knew, was a bad omen.

Part of the trouble, he decided, lay in their surroundings. After every other forum had been rejected, agreement had been reached on St. Bernadette's Parochial School itself. They were now assembled—after school hours, of course—in a room of indeterminate character. But there were blackboards on the walls, reading primers in the sagging bookcase, and chalk dust in the air. It would not have been unbearably surprising if somebody had burst into a recitation of the multiplication table. The atmosphere was not conducive to mature deliberation. Sooner or later the parents would break. Even now, Horvath's air of preternatural calm barely disguised subterranean rumblings. Mrs. Foster was ominously shuffling an array of statistical information. True, Mr. and Mrs. Ianello were both bright-eyed with interest. But they were sitting on chairs eight inches below the adult standard. This was bound to get on their nerves.

Fortunately it was Francis Omara who first took the floor. He shared with Monsignor Miles an ability to carry his professional composure into unlikely environments. He was almost too detached. He acknowledged introductions and automatically tossed the ball back into the other court.

"We have come here at your request, Monsignor, but also very willingly. I won't deny that we're hoping this means His Eminence has had a change of heart."

If any of his colleagues shared his hopes, it did not show. The only emotion Thatcher discerned was an involuntary nod from Willard Ericson. This, he guessed, signified approval of the opening gambit.

Monsignor Miles led from strength. "I am afraid that is not the case, and it would be wrong of me to encourage any such possibility. There can be no change in Cardinal Devlin's position. He very carefully considered all aspects of this situation before leaving for Rome. I assure you that it was with the greatest reluctance that he came to the conclusion

that it is financially impossible to continue St. Bernadette's.
Of course he knew that this decision would sadden you. It
would be a blow to any parish. What he did not anticipate
was that you would refuse to share with him a realization
of the stern necessities operating here. In view of your unprecedented action in seeking an injunction against the
archdiocese, I am convinced that your refusal stems from a
failure to understand. Now, I mean no reproach." He held
up a calming hand. "On the contrary. It has been my duty
to explain to you His Eminence's decision. If there has been
a failure of communication, then the error is mine. All I
ask is your indulgence while I review the underlying facts."

The parents were politely attentive and silent. Thatcher
began to revise his views of amateurs. Or rather, he decided
that Omara and Mrs. Foster, obviously calling the signals,
were not total amateurs. Mrs. Foster was clearly reserving
her fire. Omara might have been thinking of something else.

Undeterred, Miles launched into the history of St. Bernadette's, with particular attention to the long period in which
it drew on teaching nuns for its entire staff. Then came the
lay teacher, the organization of the Lay Teachers Union,
and the last salary negotiations. He referred to the growing
school population. He concluded with a plea for understanding of the official position.

"It is impossible for St. Bernadette's to continue providing education as it has in the past. We must therefore look
to the future. The school will have to be closed and disposed of. The archdiocese presently has an attractive offer
for the property. We shall continue to carry out our obligation to make available the best possible religious instruc-
tion after hours. In order to fulfill that obligation we must
take advantage of this offer. I have asked Mr. Unger to be
present so that he can explain his position to you."

Dick Unger spoke up on cue. "I know this is basically
your problem. All I can do is explain things from my side.
The location of the parochial school is excellent for an
apartment building. There aren't many good sites left in the
city. And I think I can promise you that our building will
help upgrade your whole community and raise your property
values. But I don't plan to get involved in a civil war. I'm

not going to send in the wreckers if you parents are lying
down in their path. Whether or not the school closes is up
to you. All I can tell you is that I don't honestly think
you'll get a better offer than mine. And my offer won't stay
open forever. I can't afford to run my business that way.
Mr. Thatcher from the Sloan probably feels the same."

Thus summoned, Thatcher solemnly agreed that the Sloan
would not tie up mortgage money indefinitely. To show he
was on the side of the angels—though their precise location
was growing more obscure by the moment—he agreed that
he was against sending wreckers over a living rampart of
human bodies.

Monsignor Miles thanked them both and said he thought
that fairly covered the situation. He had spoken fluently,
cogently and persuasively. But not persuasively enough.

Francis Omara emerged from some private meditation
and shook his head sadly. "I cannot agree that we have
covered the entire situation. Not when we have dispensed
with all reference to the Baltimore Council, which imposed
on us the sacred obligation to provide *near each church, a
parochial school.* I can remember my grandparents telling
the story of the tithing in this very parish to build St. Bernadette's. They did not regard the existence of a Catholic
school as something to be settled on grounds of financial
difficulty—and neither do we! But of course we recognize
the problem. And Mrs. Foster has gathered together some
of the data we feel should be considered. All I ask"—and
here Omara's mobile face was lit by a sudden grin—"is your
indulgence for her material."

Mary Foster's speech was designed to kill forever the
assumption that the Parents League did not understand the
situation. In essence, she was providing alternatives to the
sale of St. Bernadette's. She reviewed the cases in the Mid-
west where Catholic schools shared facilities with public
schools, thereby economizing on laboratories, audio-visual
aids and workshops. She described the accommodations possible under this scheme. She produced figures. Unemo-
tionally, she remarked that other archdioceses had taken
two or three years to solve a problem disposed of by Cardinal Devlin almost overnight. She went on to outline the

possibility of leasing the school building to the parents. She hinted at mutual assistance arrangements with other parishes, before they went down one by one.

To his eternal credit, Monsignor Miles not only heard her with every evidence of courteous attention, but quelled an intemperate response on the part of Henry Stonor. Stonor seemed to regard comparisons with other archdioceses as hitting below the belt.

"I am pleased, of course, to learn that you have devoted so much serious attention to this problem," the Monsignor said, wresting the reins of conversation from his impetuous subordinate. "And startled too, I will confess. I can only regret that you were unable to discuss some of these suggestions with His Eminence before an irrevocable decision was made. And I do sincerely hope that, now that he has spoken, you will bring the same thoughtful consideration to the problems which will face us in the future. At the moment, even if you have difficulty in agreeing, you will at least see that this action has been taken in good faith, with the well-being of the parish firmly in mind."

"Well, I don't!"

It would, Thatcher saw, be as easy to stop a runaway horse as silence Bob Horvath at this juncture. He was squared up to the table, his big body leaning forward earnestly.

"It's like Mary Foster says. This decision wasn't made as part of the big picture. You want to close down our school. But new Catholic schools are being built right this minute out in the suburbs. And they don't have problems in their public schools the way we do. There's just as big a shortage of teaching nuns for them. And they don't even have buildings or land. They've got to start from scratch. But nobody talks about their sharing with anybody. Somehow they can have a school and we can't. God knows we need it more. It's hard to see where our well-being comes in."

Rebellion, once manifest, is contagious.

"That's just it," Pat Ianello said, her hair bouncing with the vigor of her speech. "It isn't fair. We've always had a parochial school. St. Bernadette's means something to the people of this parish. More than a new school could mean to anybody. And even if it's difficult to keep it going, I don't see that that's a reason to stop."

Like a good commander, Francis Omara came to the support of his troops. His earlier abstraction was now discarded and he spoke earnestly.

"We don't mean that the suburbs shouldn't have their new schools. That's what progress is. But we cannot measure a moral obligation in terms of dollars and cents. I deeply regret offending anyone here, but I am shocked to hear a discussion of Catholic education based entirely on wages and maintenance costs. And it's not just this discussion that we're having here that shocks me. I can't believe it—not without proof, I can't—that there are people actually hoping to profit from the closing of our school. And I do not appreciate this fine talk about how a high-rise apartment will upgrade Flensburg and raise property values. You cannot," he declaimed, "upgrade a community that has lost its soul!"

Monsignor Miles did not address himself to the last challenge—and wisely so, in Thatcher's opinion. Instead he chose to become Dick Unger's advocate.

"Mr. Omara, I make every allowance for your feelings, and in many ways they are commendable. But I have asked Mr. Unger here as my guest, and I cannot have him victimized by our disagreements. Whatever the merits of your position, or of my position, whatever failure of responsibility you or I have displayed, Mr. Unger has never undertaken any duty toward St. Bernadette's."

For the first time, Omara showed signs of anger. "I don't think we have to worry about Mr. Unger being a victim. The real victims are the children going to St. Bernadette's. We should be thinking about them. That's our duty. Not to be thinking about the dollars and cents that can be wrung out of the parish, not to be thinking about the money that can be made when fine apartments and shops come to Flensburg."

Dick Unger had thought of himself as an observer. He was stung to find himself on the firing line. "Look, I'm in the real estate business. Just the way you're in the undertaking business. It would be a fine thing for the parish if everybody could be buried for free, but that's not the way

Omara's Funeral Home works. And you're in no position to expect Unger Realty to work any differently. I'm sorry about your problems, but you'll have to live with the idea that we make a profit out of real estate deals. And it's an idea you know all about."

Surprisingly this frank speech did not incense Omara. Almost as if he had not heard, he addressed himself to the Monsignor.

"It's not Mr. Unger's little profits I was referring to," he said, rising above four million dollars with large disdain. "Mr. Unger has been completely open with us. Unlike some I could name. As you say, he is not abdicating a duty. But those who do have a duty will have to pay for their hypocrisy. Because this Parents League is unalterably committed to the continuation of St. Bernadette's. In one form or another. We are prepared to bear the burden of changing times. And I think you will find that most people in the parish stand ready to support us in court. I can only say I am sorry we have to take our troubles to an alien tribunal."

This time Monsignor Miles made no attempt to restrain his associate. Perhaps he wanted to see if a dose of the church militant would do any good.

"You may well be sorry, Mr. Omara," said Henry Stonor severely. "For a man who condemns hypocrisy, you should take into consideration that your lawsuit cannot be successful. No one can deny the Archbishop's right to dispose of diocesan property. You will merely invite unsavory publicity and ignorant attacks on the Church. That is all you can hope to accomplish, and it is not a goal worthy of a man who professes to deal in moral issues."

The speech was certainly intended as a denunciation. It brought red spots to Francis Omara's cheeks. Unfortunately, it also flushed the enthusiast in the group.

"Now there," said Willard Ericson, "I think you may be a little hasty, Mr. Stonor. Mr. Omara can hope to accomplish much more. That is, if he is prepared to make full use of the judicial and legislative processes of the State of New York. After all, we have barely scratched at the courses of action open to him. Has he, for instance, consulted with the abutting property owners? Property that has been dedicated to charitable and educational uses may well have peculiar characteristics. Have these property owners acted in reliance on these characteristics? Have they possibly acquired an easement for light and air? An easement which would be violated by the construction of a high-rise building? As for the question of who has the right to dispose of the property, I think you are overly optimistic in thinking that a lower court's opinion will hold much weight. It is certainly an issue that I, for one, would wish to see pursued to the highest court in the state. Or elsewhere."

The sinister relish in Willard Ericson's voice escaped no one. Certainly Monsignor Miles was looking at him in more open dismay than he had accorded anybody else. Here, he might have been saying to himself, is a real *éminence grise.* To confirm his worst fears, he ventured a question.

"And what did you mean by your reference to legislative processes, Mr. Ericson?"

Ericson returned from a reverie that all too clearly consisted of innumerable injunctions, motions, appeals. His goal, as Thatcher recalled, was to stall for time. Willard Ericson promised to be a champion staller. Little babies now in their cradles would be clutching graduation diplomas from St. Bernadette's if he were given his head.

"What's that?" Ericson blinked. "Oh, the legislative process! I do think that, in the last analysis, the courts are not the appropriate arbiters for this type of disagreement. I think you will find that a good deal of enthusiasm could be whipped up for legislative change."

Not in this company, thought Thatcher, looking at the rigid countenances of Monsignor Miles and Father James. Ericson had soared a long way beyond St. Bernadette's.

"It's been decades since the Religious Corporation Law was revised," he reminded himself. "Indeed, many people think it past due for a good overhaul. Does it really meet the needs of the modern religious community? We may well ask ourselves. Certainly a general revision would settle the question of authority to dispose of property, beyond the shadow of a doubt."

There was one thing to be said for the grandeur of Willard Ericson's imagination. It silenced all the participants and eventually dismissed them from their little classroom, having agreed only to disagree.

As he was getting into his coat, Thatcher heard Henry Stonor.

"What does he mean about revising the Religious Corporation Act? Do you think he realizes how many voters in this state are Catholic?"

Monsignor Miles looked at his subordinate wearily.

"The Catholics, Henry, are the ones to worry about!"

4

A MULTITUDE OF COUNSELORS

John Thatcher brought away only one positive impression from the meeting in Flensburg, and that concerned a man, not an issue. In Monsignor Raymond Miles he recognized a professional problem-solver. No doubt the man had other, more priestly, attributes. But, despite his cloth, Miles was unmistakably the servant of a large and important institution. That this was the Roman Catholic Church was not particularly pertinent. In matters non-spiritual, large institutions resemble each other more than they differ. While Willard Ericson prepared his case, while Francis Omara and the committee canvassed the parish, Thatcher knew that the Church, in the form of Monsignor Miles, was going to take steps of its own.

Furthermore, Thatcher had a fair notion that those first steps were going to be taken almost immediately.

He was right. Monsignor Miles set to work early the next morning. First, he dictated a full report of the Flensburg situation. This would circulate among a small group, including Cardinal Devlin, before going into the files to swell the rapidly growing dossier on St. Bernadette's.

Then he breakfasted with his immediate superior.

"You're going to have to handle this on your own," said Bishop Shuster, after hearing him out. "Keep me informed."

Miles was not surprised. Bishop Shuster was a very busy man.

"Three hundred sisters threatening to secularize, Ray," he replied mournfully, when Miles asked about the latest trouble spot. "That's two high schools, four grammar schools, one convent and God knows what else!"

How did Bishop Shuster plan to tackle the Order of Teresian Sisters?

"I've got an appointment with Sister Mary Veronica," he replied glumly. "Can that woman talk! I'll just have to do my best and play it by ear. If you get any ideas, Ray, let me know."

Miles promised to do so and, proceeding to the small, spare cubicle that was his office, put his mind to his own problems. Because, as John Thatcher had guessed, Miles did serve as a high-level trouble-shooter. He was a skilled arbitrator in secular matters; he had dealt with striking gravediggers, arranged missionary evacuations from all over Africa, and organized more conferences than he cared to recall. He was sincerely valued by his Cardinal and largely unknown to others, although he had earned a small measure of fame in connection with Pope Paul's visit to New York.

Monsignor Miles stinted none of his talents in the service of his Church. On the other hand, he had vowed never willingly to revisit Yankee Stadium.

As he sat in silence, he automatically drew out a small notepad and began jotting notes. The first item of business was finding a useful outlet for youthful zeal. With a sigh, Monsignor Miles lifted the phone and asked the receptionist to send in Father Livingston and Mr. Stonor.

"No," he said gently when they bustled in. "I'm afraid we don't have time to review the meeting. Henry will fill you in."

It was not going to be that easy. "What about Father Doyle?" asked the young priest. "Is he really sick?"

Monsignor Miles was a realist. "Father Doyle is an old man. Tired too. We can scarcely ask him to fight our battle for us." He did not add that Father Doyle was probably in agreement with the parents. There is no use shocking the pious young.

". . . and Mother Superior?" Father Livingston persisted.

"The same story, I'm afraid. Now, what I want you to do is this . . ."

In a few sentences, Miles outlined a plan. It was time to organize a meeting of parishioners who did not support Frank Omara.

"Yes," said Father Livingston eagerly, quivering to get at it.

Miles watched him go with a suppressed sigh and turned to Stonor.

"There is already some mention of this affair in the press," Stonor reported darkly, handing him a folder.

"You're being too pessimistic," Miles commented. "Only an inch here and an inch there . . ." So far, the metropolitan press had simply reported the official statement released by the archdiocese. Why was Stonor complaining? Just then, Monsignor Miles came across a sliver of paper, a clipping from *The New York Times*. In three lines, it described parent protest in Flensburg.

"Only the beginning," said Henry Stonor. "If that stiff-necked bunch—"

"Charity, charity, Henry!"

Henry forged ahead. "And if the publicity gets bad, you don't know what will happen. Of course, the diocesan press . . ."

Miles closed his eyes. "I don't think we have to worry about the diocesan press."

"We do have to worry about the *Times*. Not to speak of *Time* and *Newsweek*," Henry retorted. "I'll run off a long and frank discussion of the economic squeeze on St. Bernadette's—plenty of facts and figures. Then I'll emphasize how this four million will help with the diocesan deficit. Then we'll punch how the diocese spends its money—youth centers, charities, counseling services. And I'll be very careful about the mission to the ghetto . . ."

Monsignor Miles approved the plans and sent Stonor on his way.

He himself did not have high hopes from these formalities. For instance, take drumming up support for closing St. Bernadette's. Father Livingston would arrange a meeting, all right, but Miles knew that the parents of St. Bernadette's wanted to save the school. True, some of them would not concur in setting themselves up against the Church. But there would be precious little conviction.

Except among the childless and the elderly.

And as for publicity? Sufficient unto the day . . .

Miles reached for the phone and got in touch with the Chancery's legal specialists. Willard Ericson seemed to have put them all on their mettle. So far as Miles could see, they were in some danger of losing sight of fundamentals.

"You will remember, won't you, that our goal is to sell St. Bernadette's as smoothly as possible? We do not aspire to make legal history."

"No, no!" chorused several graduates of Fordham Law School.

"All right," said Miles. "We'll just have to pray it doesn't come to court."

He wished he could believe that they joined him in this.

Luncheon provided him a brief respite from St. Bernadette's. Discussion at his table centered on television. Monsignor Kilduff had seen a rock group of seminarians called, he assured everybody in an indignant voice, the Roman Collars. Since Monsignor Kilduff was eighty years old, his companions were treated to a trenchant review of the days when preparing for the priesthood really meant something.

But once returned to his office, Miles put Thomas Aquinas behind him for more pressing concerns. Again he reached for the phone.

His first call was to a prominent Catholic layman, whose munificent contributions had already drawn papal recognition. Jeremiah V. Kinneally was also the owner of one of the largest chains of funeral homes in the archdiocese.

"Frank Omara?" he repeated after greeting Miles with respectful familiarity. "Sure, Monsignor, I've met him at the association meetings—that is, you mean the son, don't you? The old man is semi-retired these days. Father and son, they've got a good reputation. That's a nice little operation they run up there—where is it, Flensburg? Woodside? Been

there for years, you know. Oh, I'd say a little on the conservative side . . ."

Since Kinneally himself was no flaming radical, Miles
took this to refer to commercial methods. At any rate, Kinneally, who enjoyed the sound of his own voice, rambled
on without producing anything of interest. Omara was a
good solid citizen. He was a good Catholic. He was probably
a good man.

There was nothing there to help Monsignor Miles.

He frowned. Then, dialing again, he put through a second call. This time it was to a clerk of court who kept an
eye on the Flensburgs of this world for the Democratic
Party.

"No . . . no . . . I don't know any of them, Monsignor
—wait a minute, what was that last name?"

"Mary Foster," Monsignor Miles repeated, glancing at
his notes. "Mrs. Larry Foster."

"Now let me see . . . let me see. Yeah . . . I think
that's the Mary Foster who ran for Borough Council last
time around. Hey, Joe! You remember that Mrs. Foster?
. . . Yeah, same one, Monsignor. I don't know her myself,
but they said she didn't make a bad showing for the first
time out. Got a lot of friends with the ladies' groups. Sorry
I can't help you more . . . any time, any time!"

Monsignor Miles's other contacts were even less helpful.
A vice president of A&P, returning his call some hours later,
testified that the Personnel Department reported that Salvatore Ianello, husband of Patricia Ianello, was married, had
two children, and was, according to his latest progress report, one of the best young managers in the whole operation.

"He's going places," said a gravelly voice. "Not afraid of
a little work, like some of them."

"Thank you . . ."

"Going to transfer him into one of the newer, bigger
stores any day now!"

"Good."

"I've said it before and I'll say it again, a man's willing to
work hard and the system will take care of him!"

Monsignor Miles knew that Mr. Adikes had said this before. He had heard him.

"Spoiling them all with these frills. Why, when I first started . . ."

The Teamsters' Union was not interested in the hardier past nor even in the rosier future. It was, in fact, almost laconic. "Robert C. Horvath . . . yup. Pays his dues! A member in good standing, Monsignor. No, he's not active."

The only surprise that the telephone provided came from the Catholic Lawyers' Association.

"Are you sure?" Miles could not help demanding.

The Catholic Lawyers' Association was quite sure and a shade offended. No, Willard Ericson was not a member. The reason he was not a member, Monsignor, was that he was not a Catholic. He was not even an Episcopalian.

Miles was still puzzling out the implications of this when Father Livingston arrived, flushed with victory. He had arranged a meeting for that very evening. Father James in Flensburg was cooperating to the hilt by producing parishioners who could be counted on to support their spiritual mentors. Mr. Unger had agreed to come out once again. This enthusiastic recital faltered in the face of Miles's expression.

"It is only," said Monsignor Miles, "that the flesh is weak. Two nights in a row in Flensburg . . . no doubt the strength will be given us. Eight o'clock, I think you said?"

By eight o'clock that evening Monsignor Miles was instructing his driver to return in two hours. As he turned to enter the parish house, his eye fell on the bright storefront across Jackson Boulevard. The bakery and the barbershop were closed and dark. Only one store was open.

SAINT BERNADETTE'S PARENTS LEAGUE
SAVE OUR SCHOOL
A CATHOLIC SCHOOL FOR CATHOLIC CHILDREN

Monsignor Miles read the slogans with some interest. He noted the general coming and going. A middle-aged couple emerged from the store, arms filled with literature. Monsignor Miles waited for a bus to pass, then crossed Jackson Boulevard to take stock.

Headquarters of the Parents League was a bare, vacant store. The fixtures had been removed and replaced by ramshackle, battered tables and folding chairs. Along the wall stood cardboard boxes filled with brochures. There was an ancient mimeograph machine in the corner.

Mary Foster, who was talking to a young couple, broke off as he entered.

"Monsignor Miles," she said, sounding surprised. The young couple looked appalled.

"Just thought I'd come and see how you are getting along, Mrs. Foster," said Monsignor Miles easily.

"We're very glad to welcome you, Monsignor," she replied. Her calm earned a look of admiration from the young recruits. Happily for them, Francis Omara appeared at the back door. He was carrying a carton.

"Here are the petitions you wanted, Mary."

He caught sight of Miles but did not break stride. Depositing his burden on a table, he came forward to greet him.

"This is a very considerable operation you have here," Miles commented.

"Yes, Monsignor," Omara replied soberly. "We're trying to contact everybody in the parish, you see."

From behind Miles there was a gasp. One of the young people, he guessed.

Mrs. Foster's voice remained even. "I'll have to be getting along, Frank. If I can just have another box of petitions?"

"Here you are, Mary," Omara replied promptly. "But I haven't finished with the master list. It can wait . . ."

"All right," Mary Foster said promptly. "If Bob drops in, tell him I'll get the press releases to him tomorrow by the latest."

Unmoved by this byplay, Monsignor Miles bade a courteous farewell to the leavetakers. The young couple was glad to escape.

He was alone with Frank Omara.

Omara was not totally at ease. "We don't like going against the Cardinal," he said quietly.

Miles nodded sympathetically but protested: "Not just going against the Cardinal, Mr. Omara. There's the matter of dividing the parish, setting people against each other. You have all lived in harmony until now. Will it be the same if you start quarreling amongst yourselves?"

Omara replied almost eagerly. He might have been waiting for an opportunity to unburden himself. "It's a painful thing for me, Monsignor. These are my people, we have all worked with each other. But I must do what is right. And I cannot help feeling wounded. I know I shouldn't let that influence me, but a man has his pride."

Monsignor Miles did not receive a direct reply.

"You know that I am on my way to St. Bernadette's? We are having a meeting of parents who support the Cardinal. Is that what you want?"

Monsignor Miles did not receive a direct reply.

"It's a terrible thing for one person to use another. It debases both of them. I don't want to look at things that way. But, all the same, it bothers me."

There was a momentary silence. Miles had first feared that Omara was accusing him of exploitation. Now he wondered if the Parents League appeared in that light.

"If you are truly troubled, shouldn't we discuss it?" he asked at length. Of one thing he was convinced, Francis Omara was sincere.

Omara's frown lightened. "I'd like to do that, Monsignor. It would be a comfort to me. But not now. I must speak with someone else first. Maybe my doubts will be laid to rest."

"Ah well," said Monsignor Miles. "I hope we will all be less troubled. I must be getting to the meeting. God bless you, Frank."

Omara murmured his gratitude.

Saint or sinner, Miles reflected, he was the stuff who caused the Church its most grievous trouble.

Within St. Bernadette's, Monsignor Miles found Dick Unger, Father Livingston and Father James awaiting him. With them were six nervous parishioners.

"Father Doyle," announced Father James, hurrying to

greet him, "is not feeling well. He asked me to depu-
tize . . ."

"We understand," said Monsignor Miles. His practiced
eye told him that tonight Mr. Unger would witness submis-
sion, piety and obedience. He only wished that more useful
virtues would appear.

It was many hours later. The long day was ending and
St. Bernadette's lay silent and quiet under a dark, clouded
sky. The human passions, anxieties and worries about the
school were banked for the night, waiting for the dawn.

But not everywhere.

At midnight, the telephone shrilled through the silent
rectory with the harsh jangle that telephones assume in the
night.

Father James raised his head. He had just finished reading
his office. He waited.

The phone shrilled again.

Reminding himself quite erroneously that the elderly are
heavy sleepers, Father James pushed back his chair, fished
for his shoes and hurried downstairs to the hallway, grateful
for the ugly Victorian lamp that burned day and night in
the gloom.

"Hello! . . . is that you, Father? . . . I'm so sorry to
bother you at this hour . . ."

The woman's voice was anxious and apologetic.

Father James thrust aside other thoughts. This was part
of his calling.

"Tell me . . ." he began.

But the woman would not let him finish.

"Oh, Father . . . it's Kathleen Omara . . . and I'm so
worried about Frank . . ."

"Good heavens," said Father James with true concern.

"He said he'd be home early . . . and he doesn't answer
the phone . . . do you think . . . would you . . . ?"

Father James reassured Mrs. Omara although he was none
too pleased with her request. He would have responded
willingly to any call from his flock, even from Francis
Omara. Instead, he was being asked to run across the street
to see if Omara was still toiling for the Parents League.

Father James pulled on a coat, adjusted the lock of the rectory door so he could return, and set forth. Headquarters of the Parents League, he saw with disapproval, was still open. Lights blazed.

Shivering in the cold, Father James unconsciously lengthened his stride. By the time he reached the door, he was composing a searing sermon on The Humble Heart.

"Omara!" he called, opening the door.

The store was empty.

"Omara!" Father James called again, almost roughly.

He took a step indoors. Unlike Monsignor Miles, he had not previously inspected this place of defiance. His eye fell on a poster.

WHY SHOULD OUR CHILDREN BE PUNISHED?

His expression hardening, he repeated: "Omara? Are you here? Your wife is worried about you . . ."

It was bad enough that these people set themselves up against their superiors. Now they expected him to run their errands for them. Well, they were sadly mistaken.

Father James strode to the back door and flung it open. "Omara, are you back here . . . ?"

Suddenly his words faded away. A cascade of light into the dusty darkness of the storeroom silenced him.

Father James had indeed been summoned to one of his flock.

Francis Omara lay where he had been struck down. Blood told its own terrible story.

For one moment, Father James stood stunned. Then he struggled free and dropped beside the fallen man.

Omara was dead.

Beside his body, his priest bowed his head.

5

TRANSGRESSORS AMONG MEN

Within an hour of arriving on the scene the Homicide Squad had seen enough to realize that they were not dealing with a casual crime.

"You just have to take one look at the setup," a detective argued. "The snap lock on the back door hasn't been forced. Whoever did this came in openly."

"And it wasn't a pro," the sergeant replied. "They'd know enough to realize there wouldn't be any cash here. You can see it's not a store. It's nothing but an information center. Even a junkie would know better."

"No, it wasn't a junkie." The detective's arm swept around in a circle. "Omara was talking to somebody. Somebody he knew."

They were standing in the back room, but it was no longer dim and shadowed. Portable floodlights illuminated every corner, exposing debris untouched since the last permanent tenant had moved. There was a cracked ironstone sink, a massive butcher's block and the broken handles of unknown instruments. A row of hooks ran across one wall, at the base of which Francis Omara's body lay outstretched, his right hand still clutching a black overcoat.

"He was getting ready to go home," the sergeant murmured reflectively. "He'd already cleaned up the desk and stuffed some papers into his briefcase. Then he came back here to get his coat. Whoever was with him followed. Then, when his back was turned—bang!"

"He sure as hell didn't invite a junkie to come back here where they couldn't be seen."

"And junkies carry knives or guns. They don't count on finding a butcher's mallet waiting for them."

Both men looked down at the floor where the blood-stained mallet still lay. Encrusted dirt and smashed cobwebs were mute evidence that the mallet was a holdover from the days of Herb's Meat Market.

The sergeant sighed. "Okay. I guess everything can go now. Did that priest go out to the widow with the patrol car?"

"Yes, he did. She'll be ready for us now."

Whatever suspicions the detectives had were confirmed by Kathleen Omara. She had no doubt at all about the cause of her husband's death.

"It's because he was head of the Parents League," she said between sobs. "Some people are so bigoted they hate the thought of any change."

By her side Father James, who should have looked consoling, looked embarrassed.

The detectives already knew about the Parents League. They had had time to read one of the handouts. They asked if Omara had any other worries—politics, union troubles, gambling debts?

"You don't understand," the widow wailed. "Frank wasn't like that. He was an easygoing man. He didn't get involved in a lot of outside activities. He ran his business and tried to spend his spare time home with us. It was because he was so terribly concerned that he started the League. Oh, if only he never had!"

But why, they asked with kindly insistence, did she suppose the League had led to his death?

"Because he was terribly disturbed after the meeting yesterday. He told me so himself. Frank was such a good man—sometimes it was a terrible handicap to him. He didn't understand how other people could feel differently. But he said he wasn't going to stand for what someone was doing to St. Bernadette's. He was going to give them a chance to explain. Then he couldn't keep silent any more."

The detectives persisted but they learned nothing more. Kathleen Omara's information boiled down to one fact. Frank Omara had determined to speak with someone just before his murder.

Father James followed the detectives to the Omara front door, stepping awkwardly aside to let a tearful aunt and two nieces enter.

"I wouldn't . . . that is . . ."

The detectives waited patiently.

Father James steeled himself. "I wouldn't pay too much attention to what Mrs. Omara says now. The poor woman is distraught. She doesn't know what she's saying."

The detectives exchanged glances.

"Sure, Father. Well, thanks. And good night to you."

Father James watched them leave, a bleak look around his young eyes.

News of Frank Omara's murder reached the Sloan early the next morning. Thatcher arrived at his office to find two detectives awaiting him. In the background, Miss Corsa looked censorious.

"Just a few minutes," said one of them.

In point of fact, it was a full half hour. At least, Thatcher thought, as he recapitulated his one and only encounter with Omara, this was deferring other evils. It was a moot point as to which was the better way to start a day: murder in Flensburg or the collapse of National University Research, Inc.

"Yes, I heard it on the radio," he said. "I assumed it was burglary . . ."

The younger detective leaned forward. "There's a lot riding on this St. Bernadette's fight, isn't there?"

Thatcher agreed that there was.

"Money," said the specialist. "And a lot of bad feelings."

"Well, yes," said Thatcher.

"That's good enough for murder any day," said the police, departing.

So Thatcher was not surprised when Dick Unger turned up later in the morning, incapable of keeping his mind on business. He was, in fact, white around the nostrils.

"I don't see what you're so upset about," Thatcher remarked. "Of course, it's unpleasant to learn what happened to Omara—"

Unger interrupted him unceremoniously.

"Where were you last night?"

"At a dinner and meeting of economic forecasters," Thatcher replied. "But . . ."

"No wonder you're not upset," Unger said petulantly. "I was in Flensburg! Leaving the rectory across the street from the scene of the murder. At just about the right time!"

Thatcher refused to be stampeded. "Several thousand people were in Flensburg last night. I don't see why you expect the police to single you out."

"Because they've got some screwy version of that meeting we had with Omara." Unger had shed his languid elegance. "They think I said this was the opportunity of a lifetime. And Omara said he'd die before he let me make money out of that school. The explanation is simple to the police. I saw an obstacle and removed it!"

"You're losing your sense of proportion," Thatcher told him. "After all, you've been in the real estate business for years without gunning your way to success. If the police don't know it yet, they soon will."

"Do you know what they wanted from me? They wanted a list of all our past purchases! I suppose they're going to check to see if Unger Realty has left the field littered with corpses."

Unger's voice was rising.

Thatcher coughed. "Just as a matter of curiosity," he inquired, "have there been many sudden deaths surrounding your acquisitions?"

"No, there haven't!" Unger snapped.

He removed an immaculate handkerchief of pale lemon yellow from his breast pocket and mopped his brow.

"Then you have nothing to worry about." Thatcher dismissed the whole subject. "Now, perhaps we can talk about these FHA requirements?"

"All right, all right."

But Dick Unger did not sound happy.

The police approach to the Chancery of the Archdiocese of New York had been the occasion for a good deal of high-level thought.

"I don't know if you have heard of Francis Omara's murder, Monsignor Miles?"

The speaker was a very superior specimen of New York's Finest. He had been handpicked for this assignment with parochial school and Notre Dame prominent in his background. He was also intelligent and courteous.

"Yes, I have already been informed." Monsignor Miles's breakfast had been interrupted by a phone call from Flensburg. "I understand he was killed in Parents League headquarters last night."

"That's right, Monsignor. Probably between ten and eleven."

"It's scarcely believable. Yesterday evening I spoke to him there myself. He said he wanted to talk to me about something."

The superior specimen flinched.

"I suppose there were a lot of people Mr. Omara wanted to speak to," he suggested almost pleadingly.

"Yes, I think he did." Monsignor Miles was meticulously accurate. "But he was a deeply troubled man. I regret I did not learn what was worrying him. But I was late for my meeting." Trying to be helpful, he continued: "That would have been shortly before I visited the rectory. At eight o'clock approximately."

"Thank you." The detective had a short struggle with his conscience, then decided that if anybody wanted to ask the Monsignor for an alibi, it would have to be the Commissioner. "I wonder if you could describe some of the details of your meeting at the school the day before."

Miles complied with a virtually verbatim transcript. Pressed as to Francis Omara's accusations about double-dealing, he came near shrugging.

"Mr. Unger was not upset, no. He realized Mr. Omara had been carried away by the heat of the moment. And Francis Omara did apologize. There was no ill-feeling of any sort, I assure you."

"Did Mr. Unger say that this was an unusual opportunity for his company?"

"I recall his saying that St. Bernadette's was an excellent location for an apartment building. I don't think you should emphasize that too much. After all, Mr. Unger was trying to keep Mr. Omara from preventing the whole transaction. As, indeed, I was myself. Thât, after all, was the purpose of the meeting."

"Of course," said the superior specimen, rising. In a triumph of cunning, he had had an idea.

Henry Stonor looked up from his typewriter coldly.

"Yes, I was at the meeting in Flensburg with Francis Omara and the others," he said, enunciating clearly.

The Stonor description of Francis Omara's behavior suggested that his death might be due to divine retribution.

"About last night . . . ?"

Stonor glanced down at his typewriter. Then, with elaborate patience, he accorded the second Flensburg meeting far more approval.

"And it broke up when?"

"At . . . oh, I'd say . . . a little before ten," said Stonor.

"And you and Monsignor came directly back here?"

Henry Stonor could not resist scoring a point. "Not exactly. We had a few minutes' wait until the limousine came. Monsignor wanted a breath of fresh air, so he strolled around outside. I stayed indoors, finishing some notes."

The detective was disheartened. "So you don't have an alibi—either!"

Henry Stonor was thunderstruck. "An alibi? Good God, man, what are you implying!"

He would have been more thunderstruck if he had paused to explore the implications of that *either*. Monsignor Miles also was without an alibi.

John Thatcher, Dick Unger, even Monsignor Miles, could put the murder of Frank Omara and police inquiries from their minds. Flensburg, and a small, brightly lit shop on a dark street were a long way from their normal rounds. This was not true of the Parents League.

"All right! So I've told you what I know," Bob Horvath exploded. "But I was on Omara's side—can't you get that through your thick heads?"

The police said that they understood.

"You don't sound like you do!" he retorted. "Why don't you go after the people who were against Frank?"

They said they were questioning everyone they could find. Who were Omara's enemies, anyway?

"Mostly a bunch of old biddies," Horvath growled contemptuously. "Like Kavanaugh downstairs. He's always trying to stir up trouble."

They were interested now.

"Who does he stir it up with?"

For the first time, Horvath became evasive. He didn't know. He couldn't remember. He didn't mean anybody in particular.

"Okay, Horvath. Just for the record, where were you last night?"

Evasiveness became withdrawal.

"Home in bed," Horvath said flatly. "Ask Ruthie. I get up at five."

They asked Ruthie. Of course Bob was in bed. Where else would he be? She? Well, she had stayed up to watch Monsignor Sheen on the Dick Cavett show. Had they seen it? There was this actor, see. Oh, you could tell he took drugs . . .

Pat Ianello was too shocked to be aggressive.

"But that's awful! Poor Kathleen Omara! And with four children too."

She honestly tried to be helpful, she searched her memory, she held back nothing. But her answers were less satisfactory than those of Bob Horvath. She could not confine herself to being responsive. Inevitably her replies broadened into forebodings.

"I don't know what's going to happen to us here," she predicted sadly. "Feelings were beginning to run high already. But now! It'll be a matter of people being with us or against us. We were trying to keep everybody in the parish together, but this will split them apart. I'm afraid to think of what St. Bernadette's is going to be like."

By now, the police had had a bellyful of feelings.

"And you, Mrs. Ianello? Where were you last night? And where was your husband?"

Pat Ianello was taken aback.

"Well?"

"We were home in bed," she said with quiet dignity. "To-gether."

The effect was spoiled by her deep blush.

Pat Ianello was not the only one to fear what the future held for St. Bernadette's. The first reaction to Francis Omara's death had already taken place. Father Doyle was back on duty. Even if Francis Omara had died a natural death, he would have hurried to the widow's side. But now he knew that his entire parish needed him.

During his visit to the house of mourning he concentrated on providing comfort and support. He prayed with Kathleen. He consulted with the elder Omara, refusing to agree that it was a blessing the eldest boy had reached the age to take some responsibility from his mother. Years of experience as a parish priest lay behind his advice. Bereaved women did not need self-reliant adolescents around. What they needed was children dependent upon them. The blessing in the Omara home was seven-year-old Mavis. No matter what, she must be fed and bathed and clothed, she required explanation and consolation. Kathleen would not break down while Mavis needed her care. Let Peter go and stay with his grandfather.

But as he trudged back toward the rectory, Father Doyle let himself contemplate the future. He feared that the evil-doer was a member of his parish. But he was not concerning himself with the identity of the murderer—although a soul in moral peril must always be a cruel anxiety to Father Doyle. In time, he would know. In time, he devoutly prayed, there would be penitence and absolution. But now there were hundreds of others in danger of succumbing to malice and hatred.

He was tempted to condemn himself for his selfish withdrawal from the combat. But he dismissed this as self-dramatization. He should worry more about his duty to discipline Father James. The young curate had arrived at St. Bernadette's burning to join a crusade. When the crusade appeared, he had been appalled at its nature. Father Doyle had been content with preventing formal attacks on the Parents League. But was that enough? He knew he had turned a blind eye to the spectacle of Father James and Phil Kavanaugh huddled together. He knew that Kavanaugh was spiteful, small-minded and envious. He knew that Father James's defects stemmed from youth. Should he have let the association flourish? Had he added the weight of church authority to Kavanaugh's backbiting? Had he, most important of all, let Father James stray into a contaminating intimacy?

Father Doyle made up his mind. One thing was settled. Father James would be too busy to have time for Philip Kavanaugh. St. Bernadette's was not going to be pulled apart with the parish priest on one side and the curate on the other. Not if Father James wanted to stay here.

Having reached his decision, Father Doyle knew that the next step was to disseminate it among his parishioners. He could start the good work right now, he thought, entering a small suite of offices in the middle of the block. Here a small insurance agent did most of Flensburg's local business. The insurance man himself was a compound of hustling energy and total disorganization. The ship was kept on an even keel by Mrs. Mary Foster.

She looked up as Father Doyle entered but did not smile. "Oh, Father, you've heard?"

Father Doyle sat down beside her desk.

"Yes. This is a terrible thing, Mary. And I don't mean just because of the Omaras."

Mary nodded seriously. "I was sitting here thinking just that, Father, when you came in. In fact I haven't been able to think of anything else since the police left. You know, I saw Frank myself last night at headquarters. I almost wish I hadn't. I don't think I'll ever forget how he looked. At his very best. Monsignor Miles was there, so Frank was looking very dignified, but at the same time, so sincere and full of life—" She broke off to dab at her eyes. "Oh dear, he was such a good man."

Father Doyle felt for her. Larry Foster had long since proved to himself, to his family and to his priest that he was not particularly good and not much of a man. Ah well, where the dear Lord put burdens, he also put strength.

"In the end, Mary," Father Doyle said, "what better way to remember Frank than as a good man? Now, Mary, I don't want to distress you, so be open with me. I've been with the Omaras and I haven't really heard any of the details. I would like to know if you think the police are making real progress."

Mary said sadly that it didn't bother her to talk about it. "But I don't know what the police are doing. The questions they asked me were just about the meeting at the school and what I saw last night. I couldn't help them much. Frank didn't tell me anything. I just saw him for a few minutes before I left to deliver questionnaires. The police say that he uncovered something and was giving somebody a chance to explain things."

"That would have been like Frank," the priest agreed. "To give even his enemy a chance to explain."

But Father Doyle's heart sank at her words. They proved he was right in suspecting that the solution lay in his parish.

"Now, Mary," he continued, "I came here for a reason. I want to talk to you about your Parents League. Are you going on with it?"

Mary was very direct. "Father Doyle, even if we wanted to stop now, I don't think people would let us. Quite a few of them have dropped by this morning."

"I was expecting that. I want you to know that certain things that have been going on in this parish are going to stop. Your campaign is no business of the parish clergy." This statement would have come as a shock to Monsignor Miles. But it served its purpose.

Mary Foster spoke less circumspectly. "Oh, we don't mind, Father. We realize he's young. He probably means well."

"And worse you cannot say," Father Doyle concluded grimly. "Nevertheless, I think it's time the indulgence stopped. If you are going on, you—and the parish—will have enough trouble to cope with."

"We'll try to keep you out of it, Father," Mary promised. "But right now it's hard to say what we're letting ourselves in for, let alone anyone else."

6

SHE RISETH ALSO

Life, it has frequently been observed with outrage, goes on. Even in Flensburg, where Frank Omara's murder hit nearest home. The Ianellos still had to rise at six o'clock, organize breakfast, supervise juvenile toothbrushings, find Sal's freshly ironed shirt and make sure small Betty was shining enough to satisfy Sister Amelia Louise. Sister Amelia Louise had exercised a sharp eye for unwashed hands when Pat was in the first grade. So small Betty was scrubbed and brushed within an inch of her life before she set forth for St. Bernadette's. All this despite a true sense of Frank Omara's loss.

Mary Foster's children were older. Larry was not a promising Sal. Still there was breakfast, there was bedmaking, there was makeup to be applied before the invaluable Mrs. Foster opened the office and started on the mail.

Ruthie Horvath had sandwiches to make for Bob. Father Doyle had Mass to celebrate. Life went on, and so did the business of life.

On Wall Street, of course, it was even worse. The business going on was not even satisfactory. The bond market was in disarray. Industrial averages were plumbing depths that junior trust officers had thought unattainable. Statements from the Treasury, the Federal Reserve, the Council of Economic Advisers and vice presidents of all Chicago banks were beginning to sound like black comedy.

". . . while the unemployment rate rose last month."

Walter Bowman, the Sloan's research chief, met challenges with admirable gusto. The current debacle might dampen other ardors; it made Walter redouble his zeal. Just now he was reporting official statistics for January's economic performance. They had not yet been officially released by

54

Washington and would not be for some days. Precisely how Walter had obtained them, John Thatcher preferred not to inquire. He did sometimes wonder if clandestine methods were involved. If so, he would have to cover for Walter should George Lancer, chairman of the board, ever catch wind of it.

". . . but the work week is down a good ten percent," Bowman continued. "The way I see it, John, this policy is really working. That means the worst must be over."

Thatcher had expected Bowman to see an upturn coming. Walter, a huge bear of a man, had a constitutional predilection for optimism. Anyone who used the information he was so incomparable at garnering learned to correct for this, just as dealing with Everett Gabler (Rails and Industrials) meant adjusting for a congenital instinct to look on the gloomy side.

Gabler himself entered, shaking his head. "The ICC has approved the western merger," he said, in effect tut-tutting. No stranger could have inferred from his expression that this was good news for the western railroads and, more to the point, for the Sloan Guaranty Trust.

"Say, that's great!" boomed Walter, a large man in more ways than one. When it came to the greater good, he rose above envy when someone else unearthed information before he did.

Gabler fixed a severe eye on him. "It may be too late, Walter. Especially for the Duluth & Boise . . ."

While the familiar dialogue of boom versus bust went on, Thatcher withdrew to skim Walter's report. He was not destined to be given time to do so. Life may go on, but death casts a long shadow.

Miss Corsa entered, surveyed his eminent subordinates as though they were truants, and announced visitors.

"Not the police again, I hope," said Walter Bowman jovially.

Miss Corsa did not deem this worthy of notice.

"Mr. Willard Ericson," she said clearly. "And a Mrs. Foster."

She then fixed a compelling eye on her employer. Despite himself, Thatcher was diverted. There was no one more reliable on the subject of unexpected visitors than Miss Corsa.

Yet—and there was no denying it—St. Bernadette's was causing her to jettison long-established habits. No doubt it touched something deep in her.

"Show them in," he said.

Gabler and Bowman withdrew, with Everett looking as if he suspected Thatcher of ducking the Duluth & Boise. Thatcher wished he could be sure that Gabler wasn't right.

Rising, he greeted his visitors. To Mrs. Foster, who was more muted than he remembered, he murmured a conventional word of regret at Frank Omara's tragedy.

"We all feel it," she said soberly.

Willard Ericson streamlined the conventions. "Terrible, terrible thing," he said, shaking his head. "And it raises very involved questions for us."

Thatcher did not think that Ericson was referring either to police inquiries or to the difficulties now facing Omara's survivors. Mrs. Foster, who had frowned slightly at Ericson's words, explained.

"It's about going on with the Parents League," she said to Thatcher.

"You intend to continue the fight to save St. Bernadette's?" he asked quietly.

She met his eyes. "Yes," she said directly. "Frank would have wanted us to. Particularly if someone is trying to stop us."

Fortunately Ericson was not the man to indulge in sentimentality about the desires of the departed.

"Of course, the suit we had contemplated is now a dead issue," he said with unintentional brutality. "And it takes time to get these things done. So, Thatcher, I had another idea . . ."

Mrs. Foster was almost reproving. "Mr. Ericson called me this morning at the office. There's no one . . . that is, we're not sure who's going to take over for Frank."

Ericson looked at her. "You'll have to get that straightened out fast, you know."

"I know," she said sadly. "The committee will meet tonight."

Thatcher was beginning to wonder where he and the Sloan figured in this maneuvering. Fortunately, it was Mrs. Foster who proposed to enlighten him.

"When Mr. Ericson called—well, I realized that in the excitement, I hadn't really thought what would happen to the lawsuit. I had forgotten that the suit was brought in Frank's name alone." She looked at the lawyer. "Mr. Ericson says that we have to move fast—" She broke off, took a breath, and said, "So we came up with another idea, Mr. Thatcher."

Thatcher suspected that this idea involved the Sloan.

"Would you care to tell me about it?" he said courteously.

She flashed an appreciative smile at him. Then, as methodical as she had been the other night, she spoke.

"As you remember, Mr. Thatcher, we see other possibilities for running St. Bernadette's. We haven't had time to explore them all, but we certainly intend to. And we intend to file a new injunction in the name of our new chairman. It is, after all, your mortgage money that is standing behind Unger Realty's offer. Couldn't you help us? All we really are asking for is a little time."

Willard Ericson took this plea and added a twist of his own.

"It would create an unfortunate public image if the Sloan Guaranty Trust and Unger Realty, between them, were to take advantage of this tragic occurrence. Particularly when, simply by freezing mortgage money for a short time, the Sloan would be contributing to the . . . er . . . stability of a neighborhood in New York."

Thatcher eyed him indignantly. If ever he had seen a man oblivious to the need for stable neighborhoods, it was this legal Don Quixote. Nevertheless, he was in a dilemma. Double-headed blackmail, by any other name . . .

Mrs. Foster's appeal was a woman's reasonable request. She did not want the Sloan to use Francis Omara's murder to give St. Bernadette's the final blow. Ericson was more subtle, and potentially more troublesome. In these days of social consciousness, the Sloan Guaranty Trust was as much a good citizen as anybody else. And Willard Ericson knew it.

"Ye-es," Thatcher temporized.

Mrs. Foster leaned forward. "We are not really asking for much, Mr. Thatcher. It is only a breathing space—until we can regroup ourselves."

Ericson, Thatcher noted irately, looked like the cat who

had swallowed the canary. He, at least, knew that they were asking a great deal.

"Mrs. Foster," he began, "you understand that we are distressed by Mr. Omara's death."

"Yes, I do," she said, still waiting.

"On the other hand, we can scarcely let . . . violence shape our commercial policy."

She was too shrewd to break her silence. And catch Ericson saying a word at this point!

Thatcher bowed to the inevitable. "However, I do see the force of your argument. Naturally, I can't give you a yes or no answer now."

"I did not expect one. I only ask—on behalf of the parents of Flensburg—that you give the suggestion serious thought."

She rose gracefully. "We won't take more of your time, Mr. Thatcher. And we will appreciate any consideration you can give us."

Murmuring the correct thing, Thatcher escorted them to the door. Mrs. Foster might be sincere, but Willard Ericson was a horse of another color. No lawyer could seriously hope for real deliverance by the Sloan. Presumably, therefore, he was buying time to concoct new legal deviltry.

"Miss Corsa," said Thatcher wearily, "you'd better set up another appointment for me with Real Estate. We are about to waste more time on the parish of St. Bernadette's."

Miss Corsa remained expressionless.

"And I am going to put the whole thing from my mind by escaping to lunch," he told her sternly.

Lunching with Tom Robichaux—old friend and investment banker—did take Thatcher far from the concerns of the parish of St. Bernadette's. It was not high spirits that effected this translation. No financier was full of cheer these days. But as usual, Robichaux was carrying things to extremes. Today he had sent back not only his steak. He had sent back his baked potato as well.

They were strolling out of Whyte's when they encountered Stanton Carruthers.

"Just the man I wanted to see," said Thatcher grimly.

Carruthers was unalarmed. He greeted his friends punctiliously. ". . . and how have you been, Tom?"

Since there was some danger of Tom's telling him, and they did not have the time, Thatcher interrupted.

"Stanton, leaving aside the point that when a member of your firm subpoenas the Sloan, I had hoped—"

Tom Robichaux sighed heavily. "No such thing as friendship, these days, John. It's dog eat dog."

Carruthers was stung. A hint of animation enlivened his bland, correct features.

"Ericson is acting in a private capacity," he replied stiffly. "Not as a member of the firm. It would have been the height of impropriety—"

"Sure, Stan," said Robichaux, all resignation. "That's what I mean. Everybody's taking shortcuts, these days. Looking for an out. Oh, I don't blame them. But I can't say it's what I'm used to."

Thatcher took a hand. "What I want to know is what's gotten into Ericson?"

With a glare at Robichaux, who was looking heavenward, Carruthers unbent: "He's not even Catholic," he said, underscoring the point.

"He's not? Well then . . . ?"

It was a phenomenon that had been exercising Carruthers & Carruthers for some time.

"After all, John, we've had to adjust to these young men out of law school."

"Yes?"

Young men fresh from the law school, said Stanton Carruthers in a tone that would peel paint, had high ideals. They wanted to contribute to society. They wanted to do good. As a corollary, they did not wish to work eight hours a day in the hope of rising in their firms and achieving sordid material gain.

"But Willard," Stanton Carruthers said heavily, "is not a youngster."

No, Thatcher agreed, he was not.

"For twenty years," Stanton Carruthers continued, "Willard has been perfectly happy in his normal work. He has, in fact, become the outstanding authority in his field. If ever there was a man who was steady, it was Willard."

What, Thatcher inquired, was Ericson's field of specialization?

"Resale price maintenance," said Stanton Carruthers loftily. "What Willard doesn't know about resale price maintenance of rugs isn't worth knowing. No one can touch him on the Robinson-Patman Act."

Thatcher thought he was beginning to understand, but Carruthers spelled it out. Pure chance had led Willard Ericson to his first sight of wider legal horizons, pure chance in the form of a son-in-law. The son-in-law was a youthful Catholic lawyer retained to advise the St. Bernadette's Parents League. An idle remark at Sunday dinner, the benevolent interest of the older, experienced lawyer, a suggestion, a neat little ploy—and Ericson had the bit between his teeth. The son-in-law went back to nursing an infant practice; Willard, gripped by blood lust, was exploring the outer reaches of the law with the delight of a child in a candy shop.

"And who can blame him?" Thatcher murmured incautiously, thus affronting Stanton Carruthers again. To the outsider it seemed reasonable enough. You did not have to be exceptionally youthful to feel that there are more things in heaven and earth than the Robinson-Patman Act.

"You know the only thing a man can do?" Robichaux inquired once they had left Carruthers and were setting back to their respective offices.

Thatcher expressed cautious interest.

"Fight the good fight," said Robichaux mournfully.

"I am certainly willing to try," Thatcher replied. "And I think I can assure you that many others are as well."

7

A STALLED OX

Among them, as Thatcher had reason to know, were Willard Ericson and the surviving members of the St. Bernadette's Parents League.

Ericson could not attend the committee meeting that evening. But although absent in flesh, he was very much present in spirit.

". . . so," said Mary Foster, looking around the dining room table, "when Mr. Ericson called, I said that I'd go along with him. You were at work, Bob, and I couldn't get in touch with you, Pat . . ."

There was a confused murmur. "No, you did the right thing, Mary."

"Do you think maybe the Sloan will help us out?"

"That Ericson, he's nobody's fool."

Mary Foster frowned. "I don't even know that the Sloan can help much. But Mr. Ericson says that they might give us a little time. That's all we need."

Horvath looked down at large, work-hardened hands. "So we can go on fighting."

Again a murmur of support and approval.

Nevertheless, Horvath sounded dogged. "Not that I understand anything about these lawsuits." He rubbed the back of his neck in a spasm of discontent. "Hell, I guess I don't understand much—dammit!"

"Bob!" Ruthie protested automatically. Neither Mary nor Pat Ianello noticed. Both were thinking deeply. The fifth person present in the Horvath dining room spoke up.

"Of course, I'm not a member of the committee," said Sal Ianello, as thin and dark as Horvath was large and sandy. "But I think it's your duty, Bob."

61

"You're one hundred percent right, Sal," Ruthie said stoutly, pushing back her chair. "Coffee, everybody? I'll get some."

She left silence behind her. Sal Ianello and the committee had hit an unexpected difficulty.

"It's just that . . ." Horvath broke off, then continued in a rush. "It's going to be hard to manage without Frank. He knew how to get things done. And he made it easy for the rest of us. Look at the way he rented headquarters out of his pocket!"

"But we have to manage without him! We can drum up the rent somehow." Pat Ianello was fierce. "Saving St. Bernadette's would be the best tribute we could pay Frank."

"That's right," said Ruthie, sincerely moved by the sentiment. She had returned with a tray, cups and a large cake.

"Let me help you," said Mary Foster, rising. She sounded tired.

Bob Horvath watched them with a stubborn scowl.

"Why the hell would anyone kill a man—about school?" he burst out. "Who would do a thing like that? I just ask you!"

It was a question that hung over Flensburg like a pall.

Both the Ianellos looked sober. But it was Mary Foster who replied.

"Who knows, Bob? And we may never know! But no good will come from sitting around brooding about it."

"That's right," said Pat.

Ruthie nodded vigorously.

Mary stirred her coffee reflectively. "I think the only thing we can do is go on. Leave Frank's murder to the police . . ."

"And to God," said Ruthie solemnly.

In the respectful silence, the front door slammed.

"Jerry!" said Ruthie, jumping to her feet. "That boy! I told him seven-thirty sharp. At the latest!"

Still talking, she rushed off to scold her son. A sharp exchange filtered back from the hallway. Horvath shifted uncomfortably. Normally he would be fending off demands that he teach Jerry not to get smart with his mother. But normally, he would be watching television. Not holding a committee meeting.

"I suppose somebody better talk to the police while they've got our headquarters locked," he said aloud. "God, all those questionnaires are going to be mailed back to the store—what a mess!"

"It's a good thing you thought of that," said Pat quickly. "I can go down to the post office and arrange to pick things up there."

Mary was just as brightly encouraging. "And I've got the master list at my place. So we can get to work on the answers even if we can't use headquarters."

Horvath shook his head. He was a man who did not like to be pressured. And if this wasn't pressure, what was?

Sal Ianello was less indirect than the ladies.

Horvath still struggled.

"Bob, be reasonable," he urged. "It's your place to be chairman."

"Please," said Pat Ianello in a small voice.

Mary Foster just looked at him.

"Okay, okay," he said gruffly.

Bob Horvath had just succeeded Frank Omara as chairman of the St. Bernadette's Parents League.

"I still think you're crazy," he muttered.

It had been clear to Horvath, and he assumed to Pat and Mary, that the right person to take over was Mary Foster. She was the kind of woman who knew how to run things. She could talk without getting red in the face or clenching her fists. Simply thinking about going down to Ericson's office made Bob Horvath feel hot and clumsy.

Ruthie had clued him in while she was doing the dinner dishes before the committee arrived.

"Oh, I don't know," she had said vaguely.

"What do you mean? Mary's a damned smart woman."

Nobody had ever described Ruthie as damned smart, but she knew better than to let her husband see what she made of that. Instead, she had said, "We-ell, somehow I think it looks better to have a man standing up for the parents."

Horvath had tilted back the kitchen chair. As Ruthie began putting dishes away, he explained how things were changing. Ruthie had to keep up with the times. In the old days—well, maybe she would have been right. But these days, people wanted the best man for the job, even if the best man was a woman.

"Sure, honey," Ruthie had said equably. "Only after what happened to Frank—well, you can imagine what people will say, can't you?"

Horvath had not considered that viewpoint. He was ready to expostulate when the doorbell rang. And in short order he learned that Ruthie had not been far off the mark. Unanimous as they were about continuing to fight, the committee was split on the question of the chairmanship. The split was two to one.

Mary herself was the least vehement. "No, I always assumed you'd do it, Bob. It just seems right. . . . Oh, don't be silly! We all do what we can. No one works harder than you do. . . . Honestly, if I'd thought going to the Sloan this morning would make all this fuss, I'd have waited for you to go."

Pat Ianello was more forthright. "Bob, I think you should!" She was tense with the effort of trying to communicate more than she was willing to put into words.

Bob was torn. It was easier said than done—this putting Frank Omara's murder from one's mind. And much as he disliked the idea of trying to fill Frank Omara's shoes, Horvath was prey to other, older instincts. Bob Horvath, husband, father, truck driver and Teamster, came from a long line of men who knew what men should do, in new times as well as old. If there was any possibility that Frank Omara had been killed because of the Parents League—then it was Bob Horvath who should be standing up for them. Not Mary Foster.

"Okay, okay," he repeated, bowing to the inevitable. "But you're all going to have to help out. First off, we'd better get hold of Mr. Ericson and find out what the Sloan says. Then we've got to get a lot of new volunteers. Tell them it's for Frank—God rest his soul!"

Horvath still sounded truculent. Sal misinterpreted him. "That's the way to talk!"

"I'm proud of you," said Ruthie.

Goaded, the hero looked around.

"Some people still don't see it our way," he said. "About going against the Cardinal. We need all the help we can get."

There was unanimity on that point. Then, Bob Horvath moved on to new business: "As long as we're here," he said gruffly, "I guess we'd better make our plans."

He had succeeded in outstripping his followers.

"What plans?" Mary Foster asked blankly.

Bob stared at her. Maybe there was something in this business about a man's mind.

"About the funeral, Mary," he told her, surprised. "We've got to decide, right here and now, how we're going to handle. the funeral."

"You're right," said Mary, her eyes narrowing.

Nobody said anything further. Because everybody present realized just how right Bob Horvath was. Frank Omara's funeral was going to be a challenge to any number of people.

But Dick Unger, for one, was scarcely ready to meet any challenge with his usual suavity. After recovering from his police interrogation, he re-emerged as a real estate promoter. Almost as quickly as Willard Ericson, he appreciated that the death of Francis Omara equaled the death of *Francis P. Omara vs. Joseph, Cardinal Devlin.*

To his mind, the appropriate conduct for Unger Realty, the Archdiocese of New York and the Sloan Guaranty Trust was so obvious as to require no discussion.

"Don't worry, Dad," he said cheerfully over the long-distance line to the Caribbean. "If we step on it, the sale will be over before those parents know what hit them. Then they can't talk about an injunction any more."

The phone suggested that there were other ways of fighting besides injunctions.

"No, no, Dad. Once they're faced with an accomplished fact, they'll accept it. You'll see."

But Unger senior had no opportunity to see.

Almost before he cradled the receiver, Dick Unger was on another line learning that the Sloan had frozen his mortgage funds until after a new suit could be filed.

"God knows why!" he almost wailed to Monsignor Miles an hour later. "Thatcher must be crazy!"

Monsignor Miles raised fine eyebrows in rebuke. This was a signal which his colleagues and subordinates recognized. Unfortunately Unger did not.

"We could have slipped the whole thing through," Unger continued to lament, "without anyone even noticing."

Miles realized that something more than eyebrows was going to be necessary. "They would certainly have noticed afterwards," he said sharply.

Dick Unger's expression spoke for itself. "What difference would that make to the Sloan?" he asked harshly.

"I do not know, but it would make a good deal of difference to both the Church and to Unger Realty. In all fairness to Mr. Thatcher, I should say that we would never have agreed to exploiting Mr. Omara's death in that fashion. We shall certainly give the Parents League an opportunity to reorganize and appoint another chairman."

Dick Unger was still rebellious. Monsignor Miles turned out to be more adept at handling this mutiny than the one in Flensburg.

"If, by any chance, their reorganization is accomplished within the next day or two, we shall still not act. Nothing will be done until after Francis Omara's funeral. It is the least mark of respect we can show, Mr. Unger. By the way, what are you planning to do about the funeral?"

"Not a damned thing!" said Dick Unger firmly.

8

IN THE MIDST OF THE CONGREGATION

John Putnam Thatcher arrived at his office early the next morning with laudable intentions. There were many claims on the time of the acting president of the Sloan Guaranty Trust besides St. Bernadette's School. He thought these hopes were reasonable; he had given St. Bernadette's more Sloan atention than it absolutely deserved in these days of financial *Sturm und Drang*. None of the interested parties—and Thatcher had no qualms about including Miss Corsa in this roster—could complain that their demands had received short shrift.

He was immediately reminded that if there is a reward for virtue, it lies in a better world.

"What was that, Miss Corsa?" he asked. He had not yet reached his own desk.

"Mr. Unger," she repeated. "I said you would pick him up at quarter to ten."

Thatcher waited for enlightenment.

"The funeral," Miss Corsa explained patiently. "I knew you would want to attend. And Mr. Unger's secretary mentioned he was going."

Thatcher was momentarily tempted to challenge her. He knew that his age and station were accelerating the occasions for these gestures of respect. But that was no excuse for Miss Corsa to assume he enjoyed this sort of thing. Second thoughts, however, prevailed. It was all too likely, he feared, that Miss Corsa had opinions of her own about Francis Omara's funeral.

Thus, within the hour, he found himself Flensburg-bound with Dick Unger. Unger, for once, seemed disinclined for conversation. Thatcher absorbed his companion's sartorial splendor. Unger was, at all times, something of a dandy. His sideburns artfully elongated his face and his tailoring smacked of the Edwardian. Nor was he usually somber. Cheery waistcoats peeked out over his lapels; his ties were exotic exercises in contrast. Today, however, he was a muted symphony. The light gray of socks and shirt underlined the darker gray of tailoring. The whole ensemble was enriched by a tie of deepest purple.

Thatcher, of course, was in his normal attire. The uniform of banking—a conservative business suit—was perfectly proper for funeral attendance. And what a commentary on the American businessman that was!

They were speeding up Jackson Boulevard when Unger finally unburdened himself.

"If you ask me, Monsignor Miles is making a mistake," he said sourly.

Thatcher indicated interest.

"He's emphasizing the connection between Omara's murder and St. Bernadette's," Unger expanded. "If we played our cards right, everybody would forget it."

Thatcher did not agree with him, but just then they arrived at the church. The crowd streaming in relieved him of any necessity for comment. He and Unger had arrived early but still had to be seated on a side aisle. The pews were filling rapidly. Low-voiced exchanges on all sides indicated that the entire parish was turning out and taking a deep interest.

"Look at old Mr. Omara," said somebody behind Thatcher. "He's handling the funeral, of course. What a heartbreak for him!"

Thatcher looked at the front pew where an elderly man supported the black-veiled widow. They were flanked by children. But if the first pew was reserved for the family, the second pew was also set apart. It presented the Action Committee of the St. Bernadette's Parents League in solid array. Pat and Sal Ianello sat together in the center. Mary Foster and Bob Horvath were both accompanied by spouses and teenage children. Most surprising of all were the other occupants of the pew—Willard Ericson and a young man Thatcher took to be his son-in-law. Without them, the seating might be accidental. With them, it became a show of solidarity. Others thought so, too. On every side there were decorous whisperings.

"The two on the end must be the lawyers. Rita said they were coming."

"That's to show they mean to go on with the fight."

"Did you hear that Ruthie wants them to get guards for Horvath?"

"You're kidding!" The whisper was fascinated.

"No, no! She's afraid it might happen again."

An indignant newcomer spoke up. "Again? Where do they think we are? This is Flensburg."

It was not only behind him, Thatcher noted. In front of him, the conversation was running on much the same lines.

"You have to face facts. We've got some kind of kook in the parish."

"We've got more than one kind. You notice Kavanaugh isn't here."

"At least they've finally muzzled Father James. That was after he said this was a judgment."

The woman was outraged. "And high time! He said it in the churchyard. Poor Kathleen Omara might have heard him. She came to early Mass."

"And young Pete was with her."

Further comment was postponed as the organ pealed forth. The congregation turned its mind to its devotions, and the solemn rites began. Thatcher observed with curiosity the priest who came forward to greet the casket. He was an old man. He might well have known Francis Omara since childhood.

This proved to be the case. Father Doyle's eulogy opened with a reference to his long affection for his fallen parishioner. He had known him since he was a boy. But the eulogy moved on from the personal virtues of Francis Omara to his commitment to his parish and to the well-being of the people among whom he lived.

"He was ready to strive for betterment," Father Doyle said, "but only in peace. To the very last he recognized the honesty of those he disagreed with. He knew that there is no betterment where dissension and hatred follow in its wake."

From there the eulogy naturally passed into a moving plea for charity. If disagree you must, ran its theme, then take Francis Omara's conduct as a guide. He was a Christian, he was a Catholic, he was an example to us all. And we are bereft without him.

There was absolute silence at the end except for quiet weeping from several women. Father Doyle had to wait a moment to recover from his own emotion. Then he was able to make an announcement in a normal voice. The silence turned to gasps of surprise.

There would be a second eulogy, delivered by Monsignor Miles at the express request of Joseph, Cardinal Devlin.

Monsignor Miles ascended the pulpit with the assurance of his station.

"I cannot lighten your grief," he spoke almost conversationally. "I can only share it. It is natural and right that we should grieve for the passing of a good man, a sincere man."

The text of his address might have been *The Sincere Man*. Monsignor Miles was an able speaker. He did full justice to the occasion, bypassing all controversial issues. He spoke warmly of the dead man and emphasized the Church's need for concerned, active laymen. His speech was urbane, conciliatory and consistent. It said everything that ought to be said and nothing that ought not to be said.

In John Putnam Thatcher's view, it was a colossal mistake.

This congregation did not want urbanity and consistency. Most of all it did not want any suggestion of forgiveness. Francis Omara's sincerity, Monsignor Miles implied, made his error acceptable. But the parish of St. Bernadette's wanted to avoid considering error. They were much happier with Father Doyle, who gave them genuine emotion and asked, in turn, for genuine charity.

Thatcher glanced at the second row. Pat Ianello who, a short time ago, had been dabbing gently at her eyes, was transformed. Her chin was up and she glared militantly straight ahead. Sal Ianello's face was obscured, but his back was ramrod straight. Bob Horvath looked tense. Whatever his reaction, his wife had put a restraining hand on his arm. Mary Foster was the most contained member of the committee. But she too had stowed away her handkerchief and seemed to be measuring the pulpit with a cool, appraising eye.

Monsignor Miles was no doubt a skilled troubleshooter. But in this instance, Thatcher decided, he would be well-advised to concentrate his skills on handling Father Doyle. The parish priest was the man to do the local work.

Possibly Miles himself was beginning to sense this. He certainly brought his remarks to a close more abruptly than gracefully, to retire in favor of Father Doyle.

By the end of the Mass, Father Doyle had almost managed to recreate the atmosphere of priest and parishioner.

This was no mean feat as Thatcher saw once they were outside the church again. The greater part of the congrega-

tion was paying its respects to the casket before returning to
its daily round. The cavalcade began sorting itself out for
the trip to the cemetery. In the milling, Thatcher registered
for the first time how unusual Francis Omara's funeral was—
Monsignor Miles quite apart.

Children from St. Bernadette's School lined up and were
marched off by the lay teachers. The nuns were going to the
interment *en bloc*. The Knights of Columbus were also present in tight formation. Thatcher assumed that a wedge of
young clergymen were from archdiocesan headquarters and
formed Monsignor Miles's retinue. Surrounding conversa-
tions proved that some of the outsiders represented city-wide
Catholic groups. Naturally enough there was a large delega-
tion from the morticians' trade association.

After the hearse pulled away from curbside, there was a
general pause. The Omaras had taken their places in two
cars, but until they were actually in motion, bystanders were
reluctant to stride away. Thatcher had the opportunity to
greet members of the Parents League.

After suitable condolences and introductions, conversation
resumed.

"I know you're on the Cathedral's side, Mr. Thatcher,"
Pat Ianello said doggedly, "but I don't think it was right for
Monsignor Miles to talk that way."

Thatcher disclaimed any partisanship, but he did not try
to change the subject. It was clear that the Parents League
was burning to air its grievances. And Dick Unger did not
seem to have much to say today.

"I don't pretend to understand the implications of Monsignor Miles's appearance today," Thatcher went on, "but I
gathered from what Father Doyle said that it was at the express wish of the Cardinal. I suppose the Monsignor didn't
have any choice."

"He had a choice what to say," Bob Horvath rumbled.

"What difference does it make?" Larry Foster sounded
bored. "The Cardinal decided or the Monsignor did. Either
way you couldn't expect him to speak as if he knew Omara."

"He knew Frank was murdered," Horvath replied contemptuously. "That should be enough."

Mary Foster intervened hastily. "I don't know why Monsignor Miles decided to give a speech like that. Usually you give a man the benefit of the doubt when he's been a victim. But I can tell you one thing, Mr. Thatcher. He's made things a lot easier for us."

Thatcher saw his chance to put in a word for the Sloan. "So have we," he reminded her.

For a moment she was confused. Then she saw his point. She turned to her husband. "You weren't home when I got back from the city, Larry. Mr. Thatcher has agreed to freeze the mortgage funds until we can change our suit."

"That's good," Foster said.

Sal Ianello was still interested in an earlier remark.

"You mean, Mary, that people will be mad enough at that eulogy to stick up for us?"

"Even the ones who think we're acting out of turn don't like somebody from outside the parish saying so," Mary pointed out.

"And they're right." Pat was very earnest. "We're the ones who have a problem. We're the ones who'll suffer if St. Bernadette's is closed. And Frank Omara was the man who was killed."

Dick Unger made the mistake of drawing attention to himself. There was, he said, no proof that Omara's death had anything to do with St. Bernadette's.

Six Catholic parents surveyed him incredulously. Then they silently dismissed his words.

"Yeah," Bob Horvath said, as if Unger had not spoken, "even Kavanaugh will have to watch his step after this."

"That two-bit bum," sneered Larry Foster with his first show of interest. "He's just hoping to make a fast buck from that lousy candy store of his when they put up this high-rise across the street from him."

Ruthie Horvath had her mite to contribute. "I keep telling Bob that Kavanaugh is a lot smarter than he gives him credit for."

At this point, the discussion showed signs of disintegrating into a general denunciation of the unknown Kavanaugh. One voice said that Kavanaugh had no children, another that he was a born troublemaker, and a third that he was filling Father James with a lot of garbage.

But Sal Ianello rode the whirlwind and focused everybody's attention.

"He'll have to watch his step anyway," he said as one who invokes the obvious.

Ruthie Horvath was puzzled. "What do you mean, Sal?"

"I mean that someone in this parish was crazy enough to kill Frank Omara for leading the Parents League. I don't think Phil Kavanaugh has much sense, but he's got enough sense to know that this isn't the time to be advertising himself as our leading maniac."

"I hope you heard that, Unger," Thatcher remarked pleasantly as they made their way to the limousine.

"I did, and I didn't like it."

Thatcher was pleased to see anxiety on Unger's face. Normally he preferred his fellow men to enjoy life. But when a tornado loomed on the horizon, he wanted to deal with men who were intelligent enough to head for the cellar.

"Virtually everyone in that church was certain that Omara was killed in his capacity as head of the Parents League."

"They may be wrong," Unger said stubbornly.

"Granted. Although I think the possibility is remote. But what worries me is the way they assume that the parish harbors the murderer as well as the victim."

"You mean you believe what those people were saying? That Horvath will be the next victim?" Unger sounded horrified.

"I devoutly trust not. Although I should warn you. No amount of profit for the Sloan can persuade me to encourage a situation where one person after another is being murdered."

"Me neither," said Unger.

"But things are probably not that bad. What I had in mind is a situation where the parish begins to break under the strain. So far everyone has behaved with great propriety. I do not think you can expect that to last for long."

Unger chewed his underlip. "This is a lot of private gossip so far," he pointed out. "The publicity hasn't been bad. I suppose the police handouts were pretty tame. The papers haven't really played up the connection between the murder and St. Bernadette's."

"How long do you think that will continue?" Thatcher asked incisively. "Under these conditions? With thousands of people talking about that connection?"

"You think something's going to blow?" Unger sounded wary. "Did you see any reporters in that crowd?"

"No, I didn't," Thatcher replied impatiently. "I don't know where the blow will come from. I do know one thing. This parish resembles a huge pile of explosives. The fuse was laid with the murder of Francis Omara. All we need now is for a single person to come along with a match!"

9

A BRAWLING WOMAN

Unknown to John Thatcher, the match was already burning merrily in his office. And in St. Patrick's Cathedral, Unger Realty Corporation, and the mailbox of Mr. and Mrs. Larry Foster.

Protected by ignorance Thatcher was able to pass the rest of the trip back to Manhattan in reviewing what he had just seen. *Parochial*, he decided, is an adjective too often used pejoratively. The services for Francis Omara had been for a man of his parish—not for an important man in an important position. But his widow was not alone today in her grief. It was not only her church that would support Kathleen Omara, but every part of her world.

In modern America, Thatcher knew, this was almost, but not quite, anachronistic. There were still oases where human relationships had not succumbed to depersonalizing forces. St. Bernadette's parish in Flensburg, New York, was a genuine community. What chance did it have when compared to a picturesque small town in Vermont? Few people recognize simple virtues in working-class parishes, in sodalities, in Knights of Columbus. In fact, Thatcher decided as he alighted from the limousine, any visible sign of *communitas* invariably provokes derogatory comment unless it coincides with a rustic landscape.

He reached his office to find Miss Corsa, whose own community in Queens was largely composed of relatives, placing the current copy of *Time* on his desk. Since Miss Corsa never departed from custom without cause, he accepted this as an assignment.

Time's cover was so vibrantly pointillist that its subject remained problematical. Foreseeing that their message of sizzling purple and pink dots might elude readers, the editors had printed a strip translation across the right-hand corner.

CATHOLIC SCHOOLS IN TURMOIL

"I thought you might be interested in page eighty," said Miss Corsa.

"Thank you," said Thatcher, riffling rapidly. He was relieved that Miss Corsa did not expect him to study the entire article. As a steady reader of the metropolitan press, he felt he had already given schools, parochial and otherwise, as much attention as could reasonably be expected. Moreover, he had three grown children who were giving school problems of one sort and another dawn-to-dusk coverage on a year-round basis.

Somebody had to reserve some thought for adult life and activity.

He should not have underestimated Miss Corsa. Page eighty did not deal with preparing youth for life. It hit closer to home. Red lines boxed off two columns and a photograph. The photograph depicted St. Bernadette's School.

DEATH COMES TO A CATHOLIC, said the headline.

Thatcher sped through the item with mounting interest. The St. Bernadette's controversy was explained with a wealth of reference to "cigar-chewing druggist Phil McInerney" and "Sister Mary Leonard, sadly watching her third-grade class file out." Then the reader was given a powerful insight into the municipal woes of Flensburg, from tardy snow removal through inadequate garbage collection to high taxes. The knockout punch came in the last paragraph. It was a tribute to *Time*'s ability to accommodate late-breaking news.

Last week, sharply divided Flensburg was dismayed by the eruption of violence. Parents League chairman and founder, forty-two-year-old Francis Omara, was found murdered in the League's makeshift office on Jackson Boulevard. While police hunt leads, plenty of pious Catholic parents in Flensburg think Frank Omara died a martyr's death for the good of his cause.

"Oh, oh!" said Thatcher. He felt sorry for a large number of people, from Dick Unger to the Cardinal. Given *Time*'s circulation, Frank Omara, who in life had belonged to his parish, was in death going to become part of the bigger scene.

And John Putnam Thatcher had no illusions about what that meant.

Neither did Monsignor Miles.

The first issue of *Time* to cross the Chancery threshold caused an uproar.

"It is libelous!" thundered Bishop Shuster. For a moment he was at a loss for words to express the enormity of *Time*'s implication. "They might just as well come out and say we killed him!"

"They couldn't mean that!" Henry Stonor was stuttering in dismay.

"I wonder," said Monsignor Miles with a frown, "how many people in Flensburg think exactly that."

He effectively silenced the room. His colleagues gaped at him until he became aware of his unfortunate choice of words.

"No, no, of course I don't mean they think we picked up a butcher's mallet. But do they think Francis Omara was killed because of his opposition to our plans?"

There was an uneasy silence. Everyone recognized that the Monsignor wanted an answer. No one wished to provide it. Finally a lesser cleric mumbled that some people would always choose the most uncharitable interpretation of events.

Monsignor Miles's eyes were half hooded as he considered this reply.

"In this case," he said at last, "those people may be right."

"That is unthinkable!" Stonor sputtered.

Miles was sharper than he intended to be. "I'm afraid we're going to have to think about it, Henry. This"—he flicked *Time* with a bony forefinger—"makes it necessary."

Bishop Shuster, now that he was really alarmed, was quieter.

"How much damage do you think this will do?"

Miles was almost curt. "It will make a bad situation worse."

In Flensburg the Fosters were the first to see the bad news. Unlike Bishop Shuster, Mary Foster became sharper with anxiety.

"Good heavens, Larry!" she almost screamed. "Don't you see what this will stir up?"

Larry had taken off his funeral clothes and was slipping into a sports jacket.

"Things are already stirred up," he said absently. "Say, Mary, I think I'll take off for a couple of hours. You don't need me, do you?"

She could not help raising her voice. "Millions of people will read this! We're not going to be able to keep this in the parish . . ."

"Oh, it won't be as bad as all that," he said, his hand on the door.

"It'll be worse," she predicted. But he had already gone.

By the next day, unhappiness had spread to the British West Indies.

"Hi, Dad," said Dick Unger to the telephone. "How's your weather down there?"

The telephone erupted.

"Sure, Dad, we're keeping on top of the situation . . . yes . . . yes, I can see that this won't do us any good."

Again the telphone took over. The junior Unger looked wildly around his empty office.

"No," he said, "I am not making any foolish mistakes."

The phone cut in.

"Absolutely," said the son in a hard voice that echoed his father's. "I can see trouble coming as well as you can."

Forecasting may not be an exact science, but when there is general agreement that the bottom is still a long way down, that prognosis is usually correct. More trouble did, indeed, come to St. Bernadette's. It was the shape and form that were surprising.

Pat Ianello was looking in open fright at the visitor from Scarsdale sitting opposite her in League headquarters. Then, with an effort, she forced herself to speak.

"But, Mrs. Kirk, I'm afraid that it just won't do for us . . ."

Mrs. Kirk was a slim young woman with long, straight blond hair, square glasses, a shaggy coat and a floor-length scarf.

Within ten minutes, Mrs. Kirk had convinced Pat that she was a woman born to manage. There, however, her resemblance to Mary Foster stopped. Mary was competent and level-headed. At the same time she was comfortably down-to-earth. Mrs. Kirk, on the other hand, went in for moral elevation. She was also paralyzingly fluent. Ignoring Pat's interjection, she continued her lecture.

". . . the modern church. Our organization is sending delegates to the conference in Holland. So, you see, we have considerable experience in responsible opposition to illiberal Church policies. We are absolutely loyal to the Church. But we will not allow ourselves to be relegated to the nineteenth century. The American hierarchy is the most conservative—even reactionary—in the world!"

Pat Ianello held up a defensive hand. Mrs. Kirk was unstoppable.

"The whole trick, you see, is to know how to mount your protest. There's where we can help. Jane Brady has worked with Women Strike for Peace, and her husband is very close to George McGovern . . ."

Pat uttered a strangled protest. Mrs. Kirk looked kindly at her.

"Why, you don't even have pickets out," she said, making her criticism humorous. "That's no way to get anywhere—"

"Mrs. Kirk," Pat finally managed to say, "we do not want pickets. Would you please tell those women out there to go away? Thank you very much, but go away!"

Her voice rose dangerously.

"Oh no," said Mrs. Kirk serenely. "We're here to help, and we're going to help."

She was outweighed, Pat knew. She looked yearningly at the telephone. If ever she needed help, it was now. And not the variety Mrs. Kirk was offering.

For pacing slowly up and down across the street, in front of St. Bernadette's, were ten of Mrs. Kirk's cohorts. Like her, they wore hairy outerwear and came from socially aware suburbs. But it was not goatskin jackets that were halting traffic on Jackson Boulevard. It was the placards.

CATHOLIC WOMEN FOR BIRTH CONTROL
MODERN FLENSBURG WANTS A MODERN CHURCH
CAN THIS ISSUE BE DECIDED BY PRIESTS?
PLANNING IS NO SIN

"Oh, dear Lord," said Pat, returning from the window to which she was drawn in fascinated horror. The sight of Phil Kavanaugh, just ducking out from confession, redoubled her frantic desire for support.

Mrs. Kirk was continuing. "Now, we are running up some informational leaflets that we'll distribute as soon as they're ready. I know you have that"—she nodded at the mimeograph machine, dismissed it as a toy, and went on—"but you'll find that professional material draws a better response. As soon as we read about the situation here, we started writing them. And we've included a lot of references to Flensburg and St. Bernadette's. That's the important thing—the local touch. People aren't interested in general problems—even in birth control or in school closing. But you mention birth control in Flensburg, or closing St. Bernadette's—and the response is going to surprise you!"

Pat did not even want to think about the response to Flensburg birth control. Instead, she resorted to a short, desperate prayer. When the front door opened, she turned hopefully. It was not the answer to a prayer. It was Ruthie Horvath.

Pat!" she said breathlessly. "Have you seen what's going on outside? Where did they come from? You should hear Kavanaugh!"

Coolly, Mrs. Kirk introduced herself and explained that her group, the National Laity for Birth Control Reform, was ready to lend a fraternal hand to its beleaguered allies. The Flensburg Parents League, she said, not in so many words, could obviously use some expertise.

Ruthie was impressed either by the fuzzy scarf or by the overly distinct enunciation.

"I don't think Bob is going to think this is such a good idea," she replied dubiously.

Mrs. Kirk smiled, still kindly. "In the last analysis, birth control and education are issues of particular interest to Catholic women, aren't they? Who has the babies? Who wants them to get the very best education available to them?"

Ruthie Horvath was good nature itself, but she could go only so far.

"Catholic women don't do it all by themselves, let me tell you," she pointed out.

She evoked only tolerance for a quaintly outdated philosophy. Ruthie then dug her hole deeper.

"I still say Bob isn't going to like this, Pat. From the look on Phil Kavanaugh's face, you'd think somebody was giving away ten-dollar bills."

Pat made a valiant effort. "Look, Mrs. Kirk," she said, flushed with earnestness, "we do appreciate your . . . your offer to help. But I really don't think that Flensburg . . . that we . . ."

But getting through to Mrs. Kirk was going to require heavier guns. Fortunately, just then, the front door opened again. Pat turned, first relieved, then dismayed. God had produced reinforcements, in the form of Mary Foster. But hard on her heels was Father Doyle.

". . . and, Father, I don't see how you can think we're doing this! We know nothing at all—Pat, what on earth is that circus out there?" Mary cried.

Helplessly Pat waved at Mrs. Kirk.

Still unruffled, Mrs. Kirk prepared to speak. She did not get an opportunity to do so.

"Whoever you are," said Mary Foster, "you get those troublemakers out of there!"

"Attagirl!" said Ruthie.

Father Doyle was staring around, bewildered. Finally he turned to Pat.

"Patricia!" he cried. "Surely you're not behind this vulgarity."

Pat was perilously close to tears, but Mrs. Kirk was made of sterner stuff. She did not knuckle under to authority—in any form.

"Those are mature and dedicated Catholic churchwomen, Father," she informed him. "We are deeply—vitally—concerned about our Church. For you to call it vulgarity simply proves how out-of-contact too many parish priests are with the problems the modern Catholic faces!"

Father Doyle paused to marshal his rebuttal, but Mary Foster was in before him.

"Look," she told Mrs. Kirk, "you have your battles, and we have ours. We don't want you. Get those women out of here!"

Mrs. Kirk was human after all. "You need plenty of help," she snapped back. "Whether you know it or not. You're twenty years behind the times!"

Mary narrowed her eyes. "Oh, I am, am I?"

Father Doyle slapped the desk with an aged hand. "You should be ashamed of yourself!"

". . . trying to maintain some liberal contact with reality. You people haven't scratched the surface . . ."

"Listen, lady bountiful. Just get out of here and leave us alone!"

". . . the whole fabric of modern Catholicism . . ."

Ruthie had wandered to the window. "Hey," she said, although everybody else was too occupied to listen. "They've got a TV truck out there now. They're taking pictures. Oh God, there's Kavanaugh giving them an earful. Wait till Bob catches this. He's going to hit the ceiling."

Mary Foster, color rising, was glaring down at Mrs. Kirk.

"Look, Mrs. Kirk," she said, fighting to be reasonable. "Surely you realize all you're doing with your birth control bunch is making new enemies for us. We're not interested in birth control. We simply want to save St. Bernadette's. A lot of people who care about the school don't want to get involved in anything else."

"May I remind you . . ." Father Doyle began.

But Mrs. Kirk was just as adept at ignoring the clergy.

"That's the trouble," she cried hotly. "People don't want to get involved. Don't you people realize that there will never be any progress for Catholics until we get rid of this ridiculous sex hang-up? How can you honestly tell people that they're committing a mortal sin if they take the Pill? How can you order a wife to say *no* to her husband? And you say that the family is sacred! And that marriage is a sacrament! We've got to get this all out in the open! Otherwise there's no hope for the Church!"

She silenced three of her audience. Father Doyle and Mary Foster, in separate ways, realized that reasoning would make no impression here. He stood, silent, angry, and disapproving. Mary, characteristically, was racking her brain for other weapons. Pat Ianello, roughly of an age with Mrs. Kirk, had just realized what *you people* meant to Mrs. Kirk; the picture of herself as an ignorant peasant left her speechless with rage.

Bob's Ruthie took up the cudgels. She didn't do a bad job.

"I can see how you get a kick out of running around getting a lot of publicity," she said placidly. "Some people like to get their pictures in the paper and get on TV. After all, we all like a little excitement. Breaks up the monotony, that's what I say. But have your fun in your own backyard. Nobody wants you here." Ruthie herself sounded rather kind now. "We've got problems enough of our own. So why don't you just go back to where you came from?"

Mrs. Kirk lifted an already lofted chin. "What matters to us," she proclaimed, "is that we do the right thing for Catholics everywhere!"

Father Doyle was trying to force himself to deal with this iniquitous folly when the next invader appeared. A stocky man entered, doffed his Cossack hat, and proceeded to hurl fuel on the fire.

"The St. Bernadette's Parents League, I presume? My name is George Carew. I represent the Metropolitan Council of Concerned Catholic Laymen. We have been following the situation here in Flensburg very closely and wish to offer you our wholehearted aid and assistance. This is no idle offer. Our mobile bookmobile has been assigned to St. Bernadette's parish for the duration. Our emergency units have been alerted . . ."

10

THE WORDS OF A TALEBEARER

The first gusts of the whirlwind of contemporary Catholic change caused an immediate redirection of most participants in the St. Bernadette's controversy.

At archdiocesan headquarters, Monsignor Miles had little time for parochial schools. Telephone and cable wires between New York and Rome hummed ceaselessly. Policy sessions met on a nonstop basis. Vigilant eyes monitored all communications media. Henry Stonor launched one countersalvo after another.

For the St. Bernadette's Parents League, it was all a rude shock. Gone was any possibility of a modest solution achieved through private negotiations. In the world of wire services and roving television reporters, a little cause was going to sink without a ripple. How could they survive? Should they seek powerful allies? Most important of all, would anybody find time to listen to them? Their problems were endless.

The most dramatic realignment took place at the rectory of St. Bernadette's. There Father Doyle, who had been a not-so-silent supporter of the laity against the hierarchy, swung around to wholehearted support of the Cardinal. For a man of his age and habits, this turnabout should have been a source of consolation. Unfortunately he was not the only priest to make a U-turn. Father James had found a new issue. And all domestic comfort at the rectory was ended.

"I know I am sixty-eight years old," said Father Doyle gratingly to an old friend. "But when that young man talks to me about the burden of chastity, it would be more polite if he recognized that I know what it is!"

Dick Unger was watching these swirls of passion from afar. Amidst all the shifting of position, he thought it might be possible to nudge a parcel of prime real estate nearer to his hands.

"I could see the Parents League was in trouble," he later explained to Thatcher. "Nobody else was paying any attention to them, so I thought it was worth a try. At first they didn't want to go along."

"You can see what he's up to," Mary Foster said irritably. "Why should we go and see this development of his on Staten Island? We've got plenty of other things to do."

Bob Horvath screwed up his eyes and studied the letter laboriously. "He says it will give us an opportunity to see for ourselves how one of his projects has upgraded a community," he quoted.

"On Staten Island?" Ruthie made it sound like Idaho.

"It's part of the city," her husband said with the truck driver's command of geography.

"It doesn't make any difference where it is." Mary Foster kept to the point. "We're not interested."

"Oh, I don't know," Sal Ianello said thoughtfully.

"We don't care about upgrading communities! We care about St. Bernadette's!"

Pat Ianello bristled in defense of her husband. "There's no reason to snap our heads off, Mary."

Mary passed the back of her hand across her brow. "I'm sorry," she apologized. "But you'd be snapping too if you'd been at headquarters since five o'clock. And before that, I slipped out of the office to see Kathleen Omara."

"Have a sandwich," urged Ruthie, who had one sovereign cure for fatigue. "Was it bad, Mary?"

Mary was not expansive. "She's taking it as well as you'd expect. It's Frank's father who was really hit hardest."

There was a moment of silence compounded of true sympathy and a little embarrassment at how easy it is to forget the sufferings of others.

"Oh well," said Mary wearily. Then, in a deliberate change of mood: "Then, down at headquarters, we had over two hundred people. In less than three hours."

Ruthie brightened. "Did you pass out more questionnaires?"

"Questionnaires!" Mary laughed shortly. "That wasn't

what they wanted. They wanted the Pill! They seem to think we've got some sort of stockpile."

Since the first television coverage of the Flensburg revolt, a good many misconceptions as to the nature of the Parents League had arisen.

"And when you come to think of it," Pat mused, "I suppose the name Parents League doesn't help."

But Ruthie was just coming to grips with the implications of Mary's report.

"Do you mean there were Catholics coming in for the Pill?" she asked, wide-eyed.

"Ruthie, they were all Catholics."

"Well, I don't understand," Ruthie marveled. "They know it's against the teachings of the Church. If they want spacing, why don't they use rhythm?"

Mary and Pat simultaneously opened their mouths, then shut them. Six years had intervened between Ruthie's two children. Like everyone in the sodality, Mary and Pat had heard all about those endless trips to doctors demanding to become pregnant.

"Some people," said Pat, looking elsewhere, "have trouble with it."

"Why don't we all have another beer?" Bob Horvath suggested. "Come on out to the kitchen with me, Sal."

Ruthie was seeing a whole new world. "Do you mean to say that there are women—women here in St. Bernadette's, I mean—who are using contraceptives?" she demanded.

"I think there probably are. And now," Mary continued with malice, "they've got Father James on their side."

Pat was indignant. "It's just like him. Who cares what he thinks about contraceptives? After all, anybody who wants the Pill can get it without outside help," she said, thereby completing Ruthie's exposure to truth plain and simple. "But you can't get a parochial school by yourself."

When Bob and Sal cautiously returned, Mary seized the opportunity to change the subject. "And Mr. Richard Unger isn't going to help us with a parochial school either. So I say we should send him a polite refusal."

Sal was not so sure.

"You know, I think that may be the wrong way to handle him."

Mary was disappointed. "Sal!" she exclaimed. "Do you care whether smart shops and expensive apartments come to Flensburg? I thought you were worried about St. Bernadette's."

"Sure I am," Sal said quickly. "I know Unger is just trying to sweeten us up. What I'm saying is this. Maybe we should be trying to sweeten him up."

The members of the Parents League were a straightforward lot. They reacted to this suggestion with alarm.

"What the hell for?" Bob asked aggressively.

"Because we have to face facts," Sal insisted. "You know what's going on. We haven't even been able to talk to Monsignor Miles on the phone for three days. Every time we try, he's on the long-distance line to Rome."

"Maybe," suggested Ruthie, "he's talking to His Eminence about us."

"Fat chance!" growled her husband.

"Nobody's got time to talk to us, or about us. We're too unimportant. What we need is some kind of middleman. Someone who can talk to Monsignor Miles and who knows our position." Sal spread his hands flat on the table and looked around for approval.

Bob Horvath was skeptical. "What makes you think the Monsignor has got time to talk to Unger in the middle of this donnybrook?"

"Four million dollars," Sal said flatly. "That's what Unger's got that we haven't."

"Ah!" It was a long sigh of appreciation.

Pat, of course, was an immediate convert to her husband's cause.

"Well, that makes two of you for Mr. Unger. But I still say it's a terrible idea to give in to him," Mary Foster said stubbornly.

"Now, Mary, you can't deny that money talks. As a politician, you know that," Horvath rumbled.

"I don't deny it," Mary retorted. "I just wonder which side it's talking for!"

"It can't do any harm to be polite to the man. I vote for

Sal going. He's better at this sort thing than I am and, any-way, I can't take the time off."

Ruthie, already alarmed by the cuts in Bob's check caused by funeral attendance and League activities, supported him immediately.

"All right." Mary gave in good-humoredly. "I agree that there's no point in all of us going. And I still don't see what good it will do."

"Did it do any good?" Thatcher asked twenty-four hours later.

"I don't know if you could say that exactly." Unger was evasive. "It certainly turned out differently than I expected. The Ianellos came together, and I was ready to do a real job on them. That complex we built over in Richmond is our prize effort. So I started them off in the office with a whole series of blown-up shots of the neighborhood before we moved in. Rows of empty stores like that place they're using for their headquarters, ramshackle houses, vacant lots that are turning into unofficial dumps."

"I know what a rundown neighborhood looks like," Thatcher prodded.

Unger emerged from the tone poem he was composing. "Yes, yes, of course. Whenever I could, I pointed out simi-larities to Flensburg."

"Not too offensively, I trust?"

"I put it very well, I thought," Unger replied modestly. "Then I drove them out to the development. Really, you wouldn't believe it's the same place. Everything rebuilt, every-thing clean, not a vacancy for ten blocks. I pointed out the conveniences of having all these services at hand. From there I moved into my big pitch. I said when you're thinking about your children, you have to think about the community as a whole."

Unger halted, apparently for applause.

"And what did they say?"

Unger came back to earth with a thud.

"Well, then a peculiar thing happened," he admitted. "They started to talk to me! They said they realized that I operated as a builder. But there were times when I should stop looking

at things like a businessman and look at them like a whole
man. That I had a stake in the communities of the city even
if I didn't live there."

For the first time, Thatcher wished that he had taken
part in this expedition.

"Who won?" He was genuinely interested.

"I suppose you could call it a draw. They agreed to tell
the Parents League what I said. And I agreed to tell Monsignor Miles what they said."

"I wonder," Thatcher mused, "if Ianello has ever considered working for a bank."

In spite of momentary bewilderment, Unger pressed on.
"But I was saving my real ammunition for the end. After we'd
been all around, I explained that a development was like a
stone thrown into a pond. The waves kept spreading out.
Just a year ago, a big shopping center was put up only half
a mile away. I said I knew Mrs. Ianello would be interested.
That was my big mistake."

"Oh?"

"I should have remembered that Sal Ianello manages an
A&P." He brooded for a moment. "No sooner did they see
that A&P than they both lit up and dived inside. I couldn't
get them out for over an hour and a half!"

"Enthusiasts, eh?"

"They started by routing out the manager and introduc-
ing themselves. The manager had just been promoted from
a store like Ianello's. So we had a long discussion about
promotion policies and the rate of new store-openings. All
up and down the East Coast."

"A matter in which you have some interest," Thatcher observed. It seemed to him that Unger had asked for everything he got.

"That's not what I'm complaining about." Unger paused
to review his misfortunes. "Then we started on an aisle-by-
aisle survey of the store. It's astonishing to me that anybody
can find so much to argue about in the arrangement of a
supermarket. I thought they were all pretty standardized."

Thatcher had ceased to be surprised at the minutiae exercising specialists many years ago. For all he knew, every
library was filled with people still debating the finer points

of the Dewey Decimal System. He was prepared to concede that it was never very interesting for the bystander.

"Does Mrs. Ianello share her husband's interest in these matters?"

"She's a shark," Dick Unger said vividly.

"A shame. So often one can rely on the wives to damp down these exchanges."

Dick Unger then proved that the real estate business does not destroy a man's capacity for fair-mindedness.

"As a matter of fact, parts of it were fascinating. Did you realize that the arrangement of a supermarket is a lot like a real estate subdivision? Instead of talking about so many feet of frontage, you're talking about so many inches of shelf space." His voice began to warm with enthusiasm. "The big problem is the amount of display space you give any single item. This becomes critical when you get to items like detergents and breakfast cereals. There, you really have to figure out your returns with a slide rule . . ."

As a tidal wave of information broke over his head, Thatcher was left to reflect that Dick Unger's salesmanship was curiously unfocused. He had, it appeared, let the young Ianellos do as much selling as he did. Now he seemed to be forgetting the reason for this visit—the all-important Sloan mortgage money.

"Did you get much of an impression about what's going on in Flensburg?" he asked.

"It's hard to say," Unger said repressively. "Things change from minute to minute."

Thatcher decided to press harder. "Tell me, do you still think that you're going to be able to go ahead with this apartment building? In the light of everything that has happened, that is."

Unger rose to depart. "Yes, I do," he said.

It was a forthright, deeply felt affirmation. Thatcher only wished he knew exactly what deep feelings it represented.

11

AS SNOW IN SUMMER

After seeing Unger off the premises, Thatcher was brought back to the workaday world by a reminder from Miss Corsa. Walter Bowman was still awaiting approval for a list of proposals for the Investment Committee meeting the next morning. A sliding market is more of a test than sunnier times. Thatcher decided to inform his research chief personally that three pet ideas must go.

Bowman was deep in conversation when Thatcher arrived at his office. Perched on a corner of the desk was Charlie Trinkam, expounding vigorously.

". . . and Catherine says that all this hell-raising symbolizes a rebirth of the Catholic Church. Of course, you have to take into account that she's not detached. But still . . . oh, hello, John. We're talking about your buddies in Flensburg. I hear they've taken up birth control now."

Meticulously Thatcher explained that his own particular buddies were fighting it tooth and nail.

"That's not what the *Daily News* says," Trinkam reported cheerfully.

Thatcher knew this contribution did not reflect blind faith in the accuracy of the *Daily News*. Charlie was simply pointing out that, for all practical purposes, what tabloids said was what people believed.

"Besides, the *News* is probably doing them a favor," Charlie persevered. "The big thing about this Catholic revolution is that it's based on social issues."

"The parochial school *is* a social issue," Thatcher replied. "And they already had that one."

"That's where things get tricky. According to Catherine, when you've got a whole spectrum of issues, you pick the one with current social relevance. What she means," said Charlie, resorting to translation, "is you have to pick the one that people are ready to raise Cain about. And the one that's big right now is sex."

"Hence, birth control." Thatcher supplied the conclusion himself. "Flensburg doesn't seem to see things that way."

"Well, they're not stuck with it. Do you think," Charlie offered helpfully, "your people would prefer abortion?"

Unbidden, the faces of the Parents League appeared before Thatcher's eyes—the Ianellos, the Horvaths, the Fosters.

"No," he decided, "they would not."

"That's what Catherine thought," Charlie said with satisfaction.

Everyone at the Sloan was familiar with Charlie Trinkam's techniques. Given any complex or novel situation, he attached himself to a woman with some claim to expertise on the subject. As Charlie was genuinely interested in all sorts of women—as well as all sorts of attachments—he had no difficulty implementing this policy. It usually left him the best informed man at the bank.

Few women, however, had played such havoc with his vocabulary.

"Who," Walter Bowman demanded, "is this Catherine?"

Charlie beamed proudly. "Catherine was a nun. Right now she's a social worker."

There was an awestruck silence. Then Walter Bowman editorialized.

"Boy," he said admiringly, "it takes all sorts, doesn't it?"

It was not clear to Thatcher whether this was in reference to Catherine or to Charlie. He did not care to pursue the matter.

"Tell me," he inquired, as usual taking advantage of Charlie's peculiar insights, "what does she say about the current upheaval? On the worldwide scene, I mean."

Charlie quoted dutifully. "She says that the reformers who talk about the Church's lack of involvement with social issues are historically inaccurate. The Church's structure is designed for involvement. But the structure has gotten frozen, and social patterns have changed. What's going on is the travail of realignment. Incidentally, she says that birth control and abortion are just two facets of the central problem of our times."

"Sex?"

Walter had fallen into the trap.

"No," Charlie proclaimed triumphantly. "The equality of Woman! She says the Church has got a lot to learn there."

For an unguarded moment Thatcher found himself wishing he could be a fly on the wall at one of these tête-à-têtes. It was clear enough what Catherine said. But what did Charlie answer?

Walter Bowman clumped in where angels fear to tread.

"And what do you say to that?"

Charlie's insouciance was undimmed. "Catherine claims that I've got a lot to learn there, too. She's joining the Women's Liberation Army."

Now it was John Thatcher's turn to admire. He had no doubt that where Catherine led, Charlie would follow. Which meant that the Sloan was shortly going to have an in-house expert on the Movement. If predictions were right, they could use one.

"After she's been in awhile," he said, "perhaps we can talk about it. In the meantime, let me make a few points to Walter."

But the groundwork had already been laid for him. Since Walter's proposals had been typed, his favorites had lost ground steadily. Charlie Trinkam had been rubbing this in before they had both been sidetracked by Catholicism in our time. Walter was temporarily a broken man.

"All right, John," he agreed sadly. Then he rebounded. "I'll have a new list for you next week."

As Thatcher returned to his quarters, he reflected that, in their own ways, Walter and Charlie were both worth their weight in gold. These pleasurable reflections were brought to a halt. A low bass rumble was emanating from Miss Corsa's office.

Thatcher had been hoping for an uninterrupted hour at his desk. Even more important to his well-being, Miss Corsa had been sharing that hope. The most notable basso at the Sloan was Innes from International Division. If Innes wanted to complain about the Sloan's posture in Chile, he could eat up an hour. These days, Chile required at least that much time for weeping and lamentation.

Thatcher approached the doorway and stopped in his tracks. Miss Corsa was in earnest consultation with a man sitting beside her desk. Only his back was visible—a thick, weatherbeaten neck, powerful shoulders, and a gabardine windbreaker emblazoned: CONNOR'S VANS ARE ON THE MOVE. This was not a common sight in the executive offices of the Sloan Guaranty Trust. Even more unprecedented was the fact that Miss Corsa was too engrossed to notice his presence.

". . . and putting the Mass into English," Miss Corsa was saying indignantly. "My grandmother doesn't understand English!"

"Hey, now!" The man was delighted. "Neither does my grandmother. She has a tough enough time with confession since she moved up from Altoona. Of course, I suppose you could say that she doesn't know Latin either, but she was used to Latin!"

"That's it!" The two of them were getting on famously. "It's not right to go upsetting old people like that—oh, there you are, Mr. Thatcher."

The man turned as he rose. Thatcher was not surprised to recognize Bob Horvath. As they shook hands, Horvath mumbled something about not knowing if Mr. Thatcher had time.

"Mr. Horvath has come to tell you about the latest developments at St. Bernadette's." Miss Corsa's voice was the deferential voice of a perfect secretary, but Thatcher could take direction as well as the next man.

"Splendid," he said, opening the inner door and ushering his guest to a chair.

While Thatcher busied himself moving a pile of papers from the desk to a side table, Horvath rambled into an opening statement.

"I don't know whether this is a bother to you. I was down here signing papers at Mr. Ericson's office and he said you ought to have a copy. And, when I told her about it, Rosie said you'd understand, so I thought we could talk about it."

The pile of papers remained suspended an inch above the table top. Thatcher froze for a full ten seconds, like the recipient of a powerful but not fatal electric shock. By rights, a thunderbolt should have instantly destroyed the office. He knew that if he ever referred to Miss Corsa as Rosie, there would be a mushroom cloud.

"Yes," he said, "yes, let's talk about it."

"First of all, I've got this paper." For a moment Horvath was bemused by the large capitals on the blue cover. "*Robert C. Horvath vs. Joseph, Cardinal Devlin.* Geeze, it makes you think, don't it?"

Thatcher tried to break through the haze of wonder enveloping Horvath.

"Ericson is ready to go ahead, I take it?" he encouraged.

"Yes," Horvath agreed unenthusiastically. "But it's only fair to tell you, it's not going to be like it was before. We've got this Mrs. Kirk on our necks, for openers."

"Mrs. Kirk?"

"She's that birth control dame." Manfully Horvath curtailed further description. "You know about her?"

"Indeed I do. Her name had escaped me, that's all."

"She's doing her best to turn this into a three-ring circus. We don't like it, but we don't want people to get the wrong ideas."

Thatcher was beginning to realize that communication with Horvath would be largely a matter of divination.

"You mean, you don't want the Sloan to think you support her?"

Horvath was astonished.

"Hell, no! Who would? No, I mean that Pat and Sal saw that guy from the real estate company. He thinks the Parents League is folding. And Father James has been telling people what the Monsignor thinks. A lot of you are getting the wrong idea. You think maybe we'll give up or get swamped or something like that. But we're not going to. We don't like Mrs. Kirk. But if we have to, well . . ." His voice petered out with distaste.

"If you have to, you'll use her?"

Horvath was relieved to have someone else put it into words. "That's right."

"And things are going to be uglier than any of us originally supposed?"

Suddenly Horvath stopped having a hard time with words.

"We've already had one murder. I don't suppose things can get any uglier than that. This is fun and games to Mrs. Kirk. And it's a piece of business to that Unger. In Flensburg, it's a lot more serious than that."

Thatcher nodded in silence. There was nothing wrong with Horvath's logic.

The lack of immediate response did not bother Horvath. He was pleased to see that his words had sparked prolonged thought. He sat waiting, looking serious and stubborn.

Finally Thatcher took a decision. "When I spoke to you on the day of the funeral, you all seemed certain that Francis Omara was killed because of the Parents League. Do you still think so?"

"I don't know what to think. A place like Flensburg, a parish like St. Bernadette's, it's a small place really. We all know each other. It's easy to say we've got ourselves a nut, but when you get right down to it, who could it be?"

"But would it be someone you know?"

Horvath spread his hands. "Look, if it's someone who goes crazy because we don't genuflect to the Cardinal, it stands to reason that we're seeing him in church, doesn't it?"

Again, Thatcher was impressed by the cogency of Horvath's reasoning.

"Then why don't you know what to think?" he asked. "You've just explained that you don't see how you can have this lunatic in the parish."

"Because we knew Frank Omara too. I guess what I'm saying is that he was killed because of the League and it wasn't any lunatic!"

Thatcher knew he could go no further. He became businesslike.

"I don't know that there's anything the Sloan can do for you. All I can repeat is that we will not commit mortgage funds indefinitely to this project. You again have a lawsuit under way. If you can prevent the sale long enough, we will inevitably withdraw our support from Unger Realty.

But you realize that there are other banks who might provide funds."

"The place seems full of them," Horvath said disapprovingly.

"On the other hand, I am told that Willard Ericson is an expert at stalling." Thatcher paused uncertainly. Did Horvath understand what he was saying? That with enough delays and enough notoriety, the reaction of most banks would be the same as the Sloan's?

Surprisingly Horvath chose to revert to the subject of murder. "The police have been asking everybody about that last meeting Frank attended. When he got all upset about someone using the Parents League. They think he talked with someone and got clubbed down while he was at it."

"They asked me about that, too."

Horvath was interested in this news. "Then," he said heavily, "I suppose they talked with Unger too?"

Ah, so Horvath's suspicion lay there.

"Yes, they did," Thatcher replied without elaboration.

"If the cops get that murder cleared up, it will make life in Flensburg a lot easier," Horvath announced, rising to his feet.

Thatcher was not sure what this interview had accomplished. Horvath seemed easier in mind than he had been. That was all to the good, of course. But as he led the way to the door, Thatcher wondered why.

Horvath paused at the door.

"You know, Mr. Thatcher, this trip has cheered me up." He had the big man's awkward smile. "With the Parents League getting to go to court after all, and with you people at the Sloan helping out—well, I think things in Flensburg may start calming down."

12

THE LIBERAL SOUL

Man proposes, God disposes.

For many centuries it was widely accepted that the course of human events was shaped by this division of labor. Then one of the bolder spirits of the Middle Ages put faith to the test. Does man propose? Hundreds of succeeding years were spent debating the proposition.

Then, probably because Charles Darwin and Sigmund Freud between them made man uninteresting, attention was returned to the second member of the partnership. How can God dispose, somebody wondered in print, when God is dead? The subsequent outpouring of intellectual thought strained library facilities throughout the world.

But the man in the street (and the man on the steppe) had better things to do with his long winter nights than speculate about free will, the categorical imperative or the natural law. Unnoticed, the population of the world grew by leaps and bounds. Finally, an unbiased witness could have made the following observations: all traffic in London had ground to a three-hour halt, airplanes were stacked up over Frankfurt airport for ninety minutes awaiting landing space, and three overburdened mountainsides in southern California were sliding inexorably into the Pacific Ocean.

Between man, whatever he is, and God, if He exists, there had erupted a new and frightening entity—the crowd. Flensburg, New York, was about to bear witness to the consequences of this interposition.

A long and unprofitable meeting with Father Doyle had convinced Monsignor Miles and Dick Unger that affairs had moved beyond their control.

"Nor," said Monsignor Miles, "is there any reason to believe that Mrs. Kirk will prove the worst of our trials."

Father Doyle, who comfortably believed that archdiocesan officials were protected from the hurly-burly of parish life, was alarmed at gloom surpassing his own.

"Isn't it bad enough?" he growled as they emerged onto the porch of the rectory and waited for the car. As he spoke he waved a disgusted hand.

Obligingly Miles surveyed the scene. Mrs. Kirk and her determined band were still pacing up and down:

AS MANY CHILDREN AS WE CAN CARE FOR
THE RHYTHM METHOD HAS NO REASON
CHILDREN ARE TO LOVE

There were a dozen of the ladies. Watching them with lackluster eyes was a lone policeman, courtesy of the New York Police Department. Behind him, parked at the curb, was a Volkswagen minibus, bright red, with professionally painted identification: METROPOLITAN COUNCIL OF CONCERNED LAYMEN. The side doors were open to reveal a table, piles of literature, and a fat man ready to instruct any member of the parish bold enough to approach. Since it was three o'clock in the afternoon, the street was otherwise quiet. Occasional shoppers emerged from Degnan's Bakery. There was even some activity at Parents League headquarters. But on the whole, it was, to Monsignor Miles's way of thinking, a placid scene.

There were, he knew, other interpretations. For Father Doyle and, if scores of telephone calls meant anything, for many parishioners, this was the façade of sin rampant and the collapse of civilization. And to Precinct 38, this unexciting tableau represented an acute embarrassment. On the one hand, there was the right of Americans to demonstrate peaceably. On the other hand, there was an affront to every decent instinct. Duty had triumphed over personal inclination and permits had been reluctantly issued. Telephone calls poured in, demanding to know what the world was coming to anyway. The clerk on duty at the station house had no immediate answer.

At that moment Father Doyle was presented with additional grounds for annoyance. A novena service had just drawn to a close. Father James appeared on the steps of St. Bernadette's. As he prepared to descend he became aware, simultaneously, of the party at the rectory and of Mrs. Kirk. Squaring his shoulders and elevating his chin, he hurried down to the sidewalk and engaged her in cordial conversation.

Father Doyle snorted.

Monsignor Miles was recommending tolerance for youthful waywardness when a rakish sports car pulled up behind the VW, parking illegally. From it, there issued four persons: one young man and three young women. He wore a dirty toga, had a shorn pate and carried a bulging briefcase. They wore saris under Shetland sweaters and carried wicker baskets. The whole quartet was shod with sandals.

Mrs. Kirk, who was not interested in talking to Father James, broke off to stare critically. The policeman bestirred himself and approached the newcomers. The single brave soul asking the Metropolitan Council for information simply gawked.

"I have here," shouted the young man, taking up a commanding position on the church steps, "free, to anybody interested, birth control pills!"

"Oom! Oom! Oom!" lowed his companions.

"With an instructional booklet! All details! Step right up!"

"Oom!"

"Hare Krishna! Hare Rama! Get the Pill here!"

Several casual passersby crossed themselves.

"Free yourself from the establishment hang-up! Find God in life!"

"O . . . oo—mmmm!"

"Hare Krishna! Hare Krishna! Here, read our literature!"

"Come find the real meaning of religion!"

"Hare Rama! Hare Rama! Hare Rama! Hare Rama!"

The young man's chant was surprisingly resonant.

"Trained in a church choir, probably," Monsignor Miles said in a resigned voice.

"Hare Rama! Hare Rama!"

"Who are they?" Dick Unger was at a loss.

Monsignor Miles was kind to the alien in their midst.
"They are, I believe, the Bhagavad Catholics. They practice
their own . . . er . . . private masses. They regard it as an
experiment in . . . ecumenicism."

"Hare Krishna! Hare Rama!"

"O-o-o-m-m! O-o-o-m-m!"

One houri kept to business at hand. "Here," she said, ac-
costing a stupefied middle-aged woman clutching a shopping
bag to her bosom. "Here's the Pill! Use it! Never mind what
they say! Why should you sacrifice yourself . . . wear yourself out . . . ?"

The shopping bag hit the pavement just as Patrolman
Curran reached the toga.

"Now listen here, you . . ."

"O-o-o-mm!"

The picket line came to a confused halt. Suddenly, the
church disgorged a dozen people, the last remnants of the
novena.

"Aren't you going to arrest them, Curran?" shrilled an
eager, outraged voice. With wattles a-swing, Phil Kavanaugh
was pointing the finger of shame at the houris.

"O-o-o-mm!" they replied, gliding in his direction. Kavanaugh retreated.

Other right-minded supporters of the status quo had not
been so piously employed. Drawn from the Galway Tavern
down the street, they had hurried to the site of action.

"Need help, Curran?" one of them called out genially.

Patrolman Curran, who knew Shorty Grimes, cursed under
his breath. Then, positioning himself between Grimes and the
toga, he said, "Just you move on, Shorty. Don't look for
trouble. Now you, mister. I want you in your car and on
your way!"

Neither Shorty nor the toga budged. Curran, losing his
temper, shook the toga's arm.

"O-o-o-mm!" was the reply. "And take your paws off me,
you pig!"

"Hare Krishna! Hare Krishna!"

Then, as if malevolently choreographed, new life exploded
onto the stage.

School let out. Magically, hundreds of children burst out-doors—small boys and girls in mufflers, clutches of little gigglers, gruff ten-year-old boys. Inevitably, there were some precocious thirteen-year-old girls, femmes fatales junior edition.

Curran was now shaking the Bhagavad Catholic.

"Listen, cut that out!"

"O-o-omm! Here . . . birth control pills! Not just for married women!"

Moving back, Monsignor Miles remained detached. "Ah, the female of the species!"

Alerted by the rising noise level, a small crowd was gathering. Also alerted were the nuns of St. Bernadette's. Three of them came rushing out of school to protect their charges. It was a richly tapestried scene, full of interest. Officer Curran was rudely but effectively manhandling the swami toward his Corvette. Sisters Columba, Mary Jerome and Philomena were dispersing the smaller fry, who showed a tendency to pick up one or more of the chants.

"Pig! Pig! Pig!"

"Oom! Oom! Oom!"

"Shame! Shame! Shame!" This was from Kavanaugh.

"Ever seen anything like it?" Shorty and his cronies were still more amused than anything else.

Order trembled in the balance. The New York City Independent subway system toppled it.

Unseen beneath the ground the E-train, in its unhurried course from Chambers Street to Jamaica, debouched its Flensburg passengers and moved on. In a large group, they trudged upstairs from the bowels of the earth, to surface at the corner of Jackson Boulevard and 69th Avenue.

Leading the crowd were four members of the Metropolitan Council of Concerned Laymen, ready to take their stations in the VW minibus. Also present were a reporter and a photographer from *Veritas* magazine, which was, as its masthead proclaimed, an uncensored look at the Church by and for modern Catholics. Toward the rear were three married priests and eight students from St. John's Seminary, all eager to give greater Flensburg the benefit of their thinking on almost any subject.

And, alas, there were also several men simply plodding home after a long shift with pile drivers. All of them were fathers. One of them was the father of Jeanette Vertuno, a well-developed eighth grader. Jeanette was looking, with dawning interest, at the packet that the young man, who had squirmed away from Curran, had thrust upon her. And at the accompanying literature. *Don't*, the leaflet urged Jeanette, *Don't Let Sex Hang You Up*.

Dominic Vertuno was a man of few words. Around him priests, nuns, policemen, flower children, reformers, and Shorty Grimes were giving tongue.

Mr. Vertuno swung.

For several moments thereafter events moved slowly enough so that Monsignor Miles was able to chart the ever-widening spiral of violence. Officer Curran, instinctively acting to quench the flames, shoved Vertuno away from his victim and leaned forward to ascertain the damage. The fat man in the VW, hearing sounds of conflict, leaped to his door and was presented with an unmistakable atrocity—a fallen advocate of birth control and a menacing hireling of the Establishment. Without further ado he flung his unmartial figure into the fray. His ineffective rabbit punch startled Curran more than it damaged him. Even at that late hour, Curran might still have regained control of the situation. Unfortunately, one of the seminarians, magnificent in his dog collar and his commitment to peace, seized Fatty's arm in order to remonstrate. A woman picket standing nearby had not been able to see the earlier encounters. She could, however, recognize Church oppression when it crossed her path. The next moment her placard descended heavily on the seminarian's shoulders.

After that, all individual movements were lost. Issue had been joined. Concerned laymen, seminarians, construction workers and lady pickets all moved forward in support of colleagues. Monsignor Miles heard Father Doyle moaning at his side. Jackson Boulevard had become a kaleidoscope of changing forms and patterns, which every now and then mysteriously froze as if a movie reel had stuck at one frame. From chaos, dramatic vignettes appeared, crystallized, then melted.

There was the Bhagavad Catholic girl who must have jumped on Shorty Grimes's back. He was bending forward like an indulgent father giving a piggyback ride to an over-grown child. She, her sari up around her hips, belabored his broad back with one fist and gave vent to cries worthy of a Valkyrie.

A robust little boy had become the subject of a tug of war between a nun and a lady picket. The women were both disheveled; the little boy, rosy with excitement, was egging them on to further displays of infantilism.

Suddenly the roiling mass ejected the solitary figure of the guru. Like an arrow, he made straight for the church steps. Possibly he was seeking sanctuary. If so, it was a mistake for him to open his briefcase, plunge his hand in and bring forth a fistful of packets. Roaring disapproval, two of the Galway Tavern contingent set out in pursuit. Baying at their heels came three concerned laymen. At the top of the steps the handful of parishioners, all women over sixty, grimly took up battle formation.

Beyond the crowd, the VW bus was performing a stately antic of its own. It teetered from side to side, going further with each swing until finally it turned over. Revealed be-hind it was the smashed window of the Parents League storefront.

Finally, all vignettes were engulfed by the maelstrom. There were placards and fists. There were nuns' habits and saris. And, from far away, there was the shrill scream of police sirens.

13

THORNS AND SNARES

American society is not without its passions. And thanks to television, everybody over the age of two knows what hap-pens when one of them erupts. Inevitably, the man in the street has become a connoisseur of riot.

Millions of people, therefore, watched the late news round-up that evening and prepared to judge Flensburg's effort along these lines. They saw demonstrators bundled into the paddy wagon, they saw broken plate glass windows, they saw one overturned car. But, undeniably, there were many things they did not see. Where were the crash-helmeted young radicals? Where were the first-aid stations with visiting politicians? Where was the smoking rubble of a burnt-out city block?

For that matter, who was Mrs. Valerie Kirk? She appeared on the screen at eleven-thirty. Mrs. Kirk, fresh from jail, was interviewed in the living room of her Scarsdale home. She was as fluent as ever.

"Yes, I've been busted. And I'm proud of it!" she said defiantly. "In the present state of our society, being busted should be the aim of every enlightened citizen."

The reporter was adept at dealing with idiocy.

"And do you intend to continue your activities, Mrs. Kirk?"

Mrs. Kirk was sitting on a sofa with two of her children. She encircled them with her arms as she answered.

"No responsible Catholic mother can have any option. We must continue—and expand—our dissent until we have created a Church fit for our children!"

Fourteen-year-old Christopher Kirk looked painfully embarrassed. His father was nowhere in evidence.

"That's one hell of a rioter they've got there," complained one viewer.

His wife was more charitable.

"Now, George. They'll learn," she predicted. "Wait until next time."

By the following day, films of the Flensburg riot had been airlifted around the world and shown from Buenos Aires to Moscow. Nowhere did they find such a rapt audience as in Vatican City.

His Eminence, Cardinal Devlin, strolling in the gardens, did his best to satisfy the curiosity of his companions.

"Yes, I think you could say that Flensburg is typical of the communities in the archdiocese," he said.

"More pertinently, we might ask ourselves if it is typical of communities around the world," argued a South American cleric. "Are we about to witness a great revolution among the laity?"

"Nonsense!" scoffed an Italian. "America is axiomatically a nation of violence. These tensions are localized."

An animated discussion ensued. Various national reactions to papal encyclicals were reviewed.

"Not local," a German summarized sadly.

"Perhaps another Reformation?" chirped a bouncy Frenchman. "What interesting times we live in!"

He had gone too far for an intense Jesuit who had joined the group.

"And what is the answer to Reformation?" he asked rhetorically. "It is Counter-Reformation!"

"You mean in a modern context?" Cardinal Devlin asked politely.

But the Jesuit had no patience with modern contexts. "I mean that the seeds of heresy must be contained before they spread. An active and militant program is called for. The dispatch of missionaries, the use of church authority, a direct confrontation with the enemy!" With a firm eye on the Cardinal, he continued: "There can be no problem more overriding among your flock."

His Eminence conducted a rapid mental survey of race relations, core city poverty and the shortage of priests. "As a matter of fact," he said temperately, "we have quite a few other problems."

"Not involving the spiritual welfare of millions!" There was scorn in every syllable.

"I don't think a Counter-Reformation would work in Queens."

Jesuits are noted for tenacity. This one continued the assault for a good ten minutes before an appointment called him away. The Frenchman apologized.

"Father Amadeus is very intense," he explained. "And I am afraid he has become out of touch while he has been away."

"Oh, has he been in mission work?"

"No, no. He took refuge in one of your American Embassies twelve years ago. He got out only last week."

Good advice was the least of their troubles at archdiocesan headquarters in New York. Close examination of the riot coverage had produced a profound sense of gloom and a total dearth of ideas.

"This won't be the end of it," Monsignor Miles said, articulating the prevailing depression.

Henry Stonor indulged in a gesture of hopelessness. He prided himself on a realistic view of the limitations of public relations.

"There's nothing effective we can do. Of course, we've issued a release deploring the entire incident. But who reads releases when they can watch a pitched battle?"

"We must not close our eyes to the facts," Miles said bracingly. "Mrs. Kirk and her associates came to Flensburg with the hope of sparking an incident. Let us admit immediately that she succeeded. But I do not think she has accomplished much by this success."

"She has dramatized the entire issue of birth control!" Stonor protested.

Monsignor Miles looked at him wearily.

"You may not have noticed, Henry, but birth control seems to be inherently dramatic. We are not discussing a minor liturgical reform. Mrs. Kirk has not brought up an aspect of dogma that might otherwise have been overlooked. She has achieved publicity. But I do not think she will do that for long merely by staging riots."

"Think of all the other people who do!"

"Yes, yes, that is just what I mean. The others offer more entertainment value. It is unlikely that Mrs. Kirk has the wit to turn her trial into a melee where she has to be bound and gagged. She's leading a movement of Catholic mothers. Few of them are these young people that everybody is fascinated by. In a nutshell, I think that television audiences will eventually tire of watching a middle-aged woman being arrested."

This trenchant preview momentarily stumped his subordinates.

"But, Monsignor," Stonor finally summoned the energy to say, "it's the meantime that we have to worry about, isn't it?"

"Exactly." Miles nodded. "Remember, we have current preoccupations on our side. Flensburg, I am happy to say, is intrinsically uninteresting. Riots in Detroit, or in Watts, at Columbia or at Harvard, are one thing. Half-baked riots in unknown middle-class neighborhoods do not arouse the same enthusiasm. Our immediate concern is to confine Mrs. Kirk to Flensburg. There, I confidently expect, she will ultimately flicker like a candle flame and expire."

This pleasing image could not fail to produce satisfaction in most of the men sitting at the table. One face, however, became more unhappy than ever.

"But, Monsignor!" It was Father Doyle who spoke. "Keeping Mrs. Kirk in Flensburg may be easy. But have you thought of the consequences to my parish? We already have dissension and turmoil in our midst. This will add physical violence."

Monsignor Miles knew that this was not the time to remind Father Doyle that you can't make an omelet without breaking a few eggs. He suggested a more positive outlook.

"You're being too pessimistic, Father. I have every confidence in the good sense of your parish."

"That," muttered Father Doyle rebelliously, "is because you don't know them the way I do."

Nothing could have exceeded the Monsignor's forbearance. He knew that elderly parish priests, left in autonomous authority for decades, become rigid in outlook.

"Too much good sense to descend to outright violence. Besides, your parishioners are not likely to want to copy Mrs. Kirk's particular style," Monsignor Miles observed.

But life styles were too advanced a concept for Father Doyle. He said stubbornly that the sooner Mrs. Kirk and all her works were out of Flensburg, the better. In fact, the more wholesome.

For a moment Miles looked thoughtfully at his fingers. The insularity of St. Bernadette's was stronger than he had bargained for. Its priest was not only remote from the power structure of the Church, he was proving innocent of more

recent phenomena—such as suburban women and pop soci-
ology. In these treacherous waters, a lure of some sort was
necessary.

"We must not lose sight of one point," he began.

"*One* point!" lamented poor Father Doyle. "There seem to
me to be lots. Never did I think I would live to see the day
when I would have to go down to the police station to bail out
my curate."

Unwittingly he had presented an image graphic enough
to silence the company. Not a man present was under forty-
five. Except, of course, for Henry Stonor. And Stonor, however devout, was not a priest.

"I am sure that everybody at the precinct house was very
understanding," somebody faltered.

"Understanding? They offered to run him out of the parish
for me! And that's a fine thing for a man like Robert
O'Connell to offer to do for me."

Father Doyle was now glaring around the table. They in
turn were studying him with respect. The old priest was
quick to sense his sudden advantage.

"And so there's one point for me to worry about," he said
with unaccustomed irony. "I have a parishioner murdered
and a family grieving. I have a parochial school being closed.
I have one riot over and others to come. On top of that, my
curate is either a heretic or a maniac, and I leave it to you
to decide which!"

Father Doyle was neither conciliatory nor respectful. He
did however convey the feelings of a man harassed beyond
endurance.

It was Monsignor Miles who was placatory.

"Father, we know you have many troubles. I was trying
to explain that some of them cancel each other."

The parish priest was openly suspicious. "That would be
a fine thing," he said warily.

"With Mrs. Kirk on stage, I think that the Parents League
will have no choice but to cease its activities. They are good
church people, all of them. When riots break out in front of
the rectory, when the convent is in danger of being stormed,
they will realize that now is the time to support the Church,
not attack it."

"And when Mrs. Kirk is gone?"

"By that time, St. Bernadette's Parochial School will have been sold."

Father Doyle was outraged.

"No, I won't go along with that," Bob Horvath was saying as the Parents League Action Committee came to much the same conclusion as Monsignor Miles, albeit two days later.

"But, Bob! What can we do?" Mary Foster said patiently. "You don't mean to say that you want us to join forces with Mrs. Kirk?"

Bob Horvath looked at her out of two very clear, very blue eyes. "Only the fact that you are a lady, Mary, stops me from telling you what you can do with that Kirk woman."

Almost all of Horvath's ideas about womanliness had been offended by Valerie Kirk's statements, actions and attitudes.

"Bob, I feel the same way you do," Mary said sincerely, "but if we don't join her, then we have to go on in the same old way. Sooner or later, she'll leave Flensburg, but we'll still be here."

"We will, but will St. Bernadette's?"

Mary stared at him. Then she looked around at the others. "What do you think?" she asked with uncharacteristic helplessness. Mary Foster was not usually at a loss for suggestions.

"I think Bob's right," Sal said unhappily.

Pat and Ruthie confined themselves to solemn nods.

"I will not admit that Mrs. Kirk has made the situation hopeless," Mary suddenly snapped.

"That's the spirit," Horvath applauded.

Mary smiled at him affectionately. "I'd feel better about it if we had some concrete plan."

"That's what we need, all right. And I say two heads are better than one." Horvath leaned back like a man who has elaborated a complex strategy.

"That's right," Ruthie echoed dutifully.

Everybody else waited.

"There are five of us here," Sal finally ventured.

"No, no." Horvath sought words to express himself. "It stands to reason if we get all of us together, we've got a better chance of coming up with something. We're not supposed to do all the thinking," he ended aggrievedly.

Sal Ianello saw the light.

"You mean we should call a meeting of all the Parents League? All two hundred of them?"

Bob Horvath nodded vast approval.

"Of course, I suppose we could," Sal said dubiously. He was all too familiar with the usual product of an open meeting. "In an emergency like this, one of them might come up with something."

Mary and Ruthie provided their formal consent. Pat Ianello, however, seemed lost in thought.

"Well, honey," Sal prodded, "you're the official member of this committee."

Everybody smiled. Formalities meant very little when a couple was as united as the Ianellos.

Pat was the only one who missed the joke. She came to herself with a start.

"Oh, I agree. Let's call the meeting. But I'll tell you what! Let's have Mr. Ericson there. He seems to be a man with ideas!"

14

COUNSEL IS MINE

"I have one or two little ideas," Willard Ericson said with satisfaction as the subway jolted into movement.

Thatcher bestirred himself to courtesy. "I'm sure you do. You wouldn't care to tell me what they are?"

Ericson shook his head. "I'd rather see how this parents' meeting tonight develops. I'll probably have to play it by ear. But you won't be sorry you came." He paused to inspect his companion. "The trouble with you people in ivory towers is that you forget how the little man reacts to pressure. This trip will do you good!"

The banshee roar of their passage under the East River made reply impossible. It was just as well. Thatcher controlled his instinctive response. Why, he wondered, was the Sloan Guaranty Trust supposed to be so much further from reality than Carruthers & Carruthers?

"I've had a good deal of exposure to how the Parents League feels about St. Bernadette's," he said when the noise abated.

"Oh, that!" Ericson became didactic. "I'm talking about something else. They know the result they want—the continuation of the school. It's strategy they should be thinking about. With riots and birth control on the scene, they have the makings of a genuine protest movement. But they lack one essential ingredient. And need we ask what that it?"

Ericson took breath to answer his own question, thereby losing his opportunity.

"They need a socially relevant issue," barked Thatcher. He had always been a quick learner.

Ericson was not pleased at this interruption. " I suppose you could put it that way," he said ungenerously. "I propose to give them the one issue around which the entire movement will cohere."

Was it possible, Thatcher asked himself, that Ericson knew Charlie Trinkam's Catherine, too?

"Tell me," he asked affably, "is it going to be the equality of woman?"

Ericson blinked. "I beg your pardon?"

"Never mind." Thatcher waved it away. "Just a mistake." Still it was a shame, he reflected. He would like to see Bob Horvath's face.

Meanwhile Ericson recovered. "I think you will be surprised at the potential for organized opposition in Flensburg. Properly directed, that is."

Thatcher was considering this statement with some misgivings as they pulled into the pandemonium of Queens Plaza. Miss Corsa, he decided, had seen which way the wind was blowing from the beginning. And was that so surprising? She was on home ground. *He* might just as well be in a foreign country. How much did he know about this section of New York? Idly his eyes strayed across the tracks. For instance, where did the GG train go? For all he knew, it might just as well service some outer suburb of Bucharest.

"I could be surprised by almost anything in Flensburg," he announced truthfully.

They arrived at St. Bernadette's a few minutes before the meeting was scheduled to open. Thatcher let Ericson go forward to join the committee while he headed for an unobtrusive seat at the side of the first row. From there he should be able to recognize any stage managing.

The crowd was large and animated. There were work clothes as well as business suits; there were pink curlers as well as lacquered coiffures. And, of course, there were the three surviving members of the action committee.

They sounded disturbed as they responded to Ericson's greeting.

"Evening," Bob Horvath replied in a troubled voice. He was watching the full two hundred members of the Parents League stream in. Suddenly he pointed to a man near the water cooler.

"He's not a member," he grunted.

"We can't throw him out, Bob," said Pat Ianello. "Besides . . ."

Besides, it rapidly became clear, there were going to be many more than two hundred people present tonight.

"Christ," muttered Horvath, "I hope we're not going to have another riot!"

"I think," Willard Ericson suggested, "we should be about ready to begin, don't you, Mr. Chairman?"

He might just as well have licked his chops, Thatcher thought.

Bob unhappily clambered to his feet.

"I guess we can—can you hear me all right back there? Fine—I guess we can begin now." He glanced down at a pad of paper with large printed letters. "Now, the first order of business is to have the secretary read the minutes of the last meeting. Mary—that is, Mrs. Foster."

There was a small flurry of handclapping. Mary Foster

rose. In a clear, steady voice, she read an account of the last plenary meeting of the St. Bernadette's Parents League.

Thatcher noted that these preliminaries were not accompanied by the usual coughing or foot-shuffling. There was absolute silence, broken only by a general sigh when the name Frank Omara was mentioned.

This obviously troubled Bob Horvath. It puzzled Mary Foster, who ended by speaking too rapidly. Little Mrs. Ianello looked as if she were trying to solve a conundrum. Only Willard Ericson was untouched.

The secretary's report was read and approved. Then Mrs. Ianello presented the treasurer's report. It, too, was approved unanimously. Then the floor got its chance.

It immediately became clear to Thatcher that Flensburg was as transformed by events as Willard Ericson. The riot, Mrs. Valerie Kirk and the Bhagavad Catholics had done what they set out to do: they had made a smashing impact on Flensburg. Not that they had won adherents to the cause of liberalized birth control laws, far less to the rapprochement between Catholicism and Zen Buddhism. What they had sparked was blood lust. The Flensburg parents did not want to riot—but they did want to act forcefully, dramatically and unambiguously. Just like everybody else.

A sane, temperate program to save St. Bernadette's Grammar School remained everybody's avowed goal. But Thatcher identified an inchoate yearning for the exhilaration of hand-to-hand combat. Everybody deplored, at length, what had happened on Jackson Boulevard. Nobody wanted to get busted. For that matter, Flensburg did not really understand why anybody would want to get busted. But stirring events have insidious side effects. The parents surrounding Thatcher had looked on high drama. In each and every one of them, something had twitched.

His neighbor spelled this out.

"Gee, Lil," she was saying across her husband. "I thought they'd send the television, didn't you? They had everybody else on TV. Harry said they were bound to. Made me promise not to give any interviews. You know Harry."

Harry himself, arms crossed, sat mute. Television cameras could have done a lot with that heavy scowl.

". . . don't want St. Bernadette's to get involved with that
woman and her dirty talk. I don't send Lucille to St. Bernadette's so she should turn out to be a bad girl, God forbid."
The speaker was tearfully intense. She touched a chord.

There was an outburst of cheering and applause.

"And them kids with the beads and the crazy clothes,"
began one father.

For fully seven minutes, Flensburg let itself go on the
Bhagavad Catholics. Voices were raised in all corners, eager
to get in a few licks on rock masses, seminarians, lay teachers
and a number of other subjects.

Thatcher began to feel that Ericson might have something with those ivory towers.

A middle-aged man at the back of the hall was on his feet,
yelling.

"Sure, sure!" he bellowed. "But where's all this getting us?
We got to do something, don't we?"

"Attaboy, Rico!"

"I agree one hunnert percent!"

"We just gonna sit here and take it?"

There was a low growl of approval from the men, punc-
tuated with yips and cries from the gentler sex.

"We gonna let them just push us around?" cried an
incendiary voice.

Horvath looked at his tablemates, found no help, then
shouted at the crowd.

"Let's all keep calm! It's not going to do us any good to
get all hot under the collar! The reason we're meeting tonight . . ."

A heckler cut in: "Yaagh! Meetings! What good do meetings do?"

Over a rising noise level Horvath forged on: ". . . we
want to know if any of you have some ideas. We all agree
that we don't want to get involved with . . . with these birth
control people . . ."

Catcalls!

". . . or that bunch of kooks with the beads!"

Worse.

"So we figured on a meeting—an open meeting. If you've
got any ideas to give to the committee, this is your chance."

For fifteen minutes the hall rang with vigorous description of personal philosophy and religious inclination. There was also much impugning of the motives of others, from Valerie Kirk to the Roman Catholic hierarchy (Father Doyle excepted). Even Father James came in for some hard words by older members of his flock.

After twenty minutes Thatcher concluded that new ideas, however you defined them, were in short supply. The whole inflammable mass was about to subside into smoldering resentment at events beyond its control. Indeed, several members of the audience were ready to throw in the sponge.

"Ah, what good is all this talk?" demanded somebody. "There's nothing we can do. There never is. You can't beat city hall."

Reaction was fragmented. Optimists protested this abysmal surrender; cynics shrugged and accepted.

"If I may," said Willard Ericson in a snappy and cheerful voice.

Thatcher saw that the moment had come.

"Sure, sure," said Bob Horvath desperately.

Willard Ericson rose, appraising two hundred plus men and women, baffled and enraged. Thatcher leaned back, prepared to enjoy the performance of a first-rate lawyer. Ericson might not know much about untroubled piety, but he was a master of adversarial situations. That which should be made clear, he would make childishly obvious. That which should be concealed, he would camouflage, shroud and, if need be, sink completely. Thatcher suspected that Willard Ericson lacked the poet's insight into the human heart. But he had spent a lot of time in court. Litigation about the price of rugs may not enlarge the soul; it does show how human beings behave in stressful situations. For are not rug manufacturers human too?

In short, Willard Ericson was a better working psychologist, when it came to controversy, than many psychoanalysts Thatcher had met. Interpersonal relationships left him cold. Ericson knew how to win a case.

He looked over his audience. They looked back hopefully.

"I fully sympathize with your strong feelings about recent developments," he said blandly. "But we must be sensible and concentrate on the main purpose of your . . . our . . . organization. That is, is it not, to save St. Bernadette's Grammar School?"

This lukewarm formulation dampened everybody briefly.

"That's right," murmured a few knitting women who had not been following the proceedings.

Mary Foster apparently felt that Ericson deserved more support. "Yes, that's right," she declared.

"It has occurred to me," said Ericson modestly, "that this proposal to sell St. Bernadette's to Unger Realty will add one more absentee landlord to a community that already has too many."

So that was the cat in the bag, thought Thatcher with appreciation.

"In my study of the situation," said Ericson, waving his red flag as deliberately as anybody could, "I have considered the proposition put forth by Unger, by the Sloan, and I regret to say, by Cardinal Devlin, that this project will upgrade the total neighborhood. Leaving aside the loss of your school, I have discovered that where Flensburg property is locally owned, it is excellently maintained . . ."

"You're damned right it is!" said a truculent voice. "We paint every other year . . . and what does it get us? Higher taxes!"

Ericson ignored this red herring. "But where there is rundown or dilapidated property—in short where Flensburg is in real need of upgrading—that is where you will find an absentee landlord."

"Boy, you got it in one," said a convert. "They haven't fixed our front steps in three years. Every month I call . . ."

"You know that bunch of stores on Jackson Boulevard," people reminded each other.

". . . this proposition that massive rebuilding, which will also destroy a dearly beloved school, is necessary to upgrade this community is untenable," said Ericson sternly.

"What's *untenable* mean?" Thatcher's neighbor asked.

Ericson did not seem to hear the growing rumble of approval.

"Now my suggestion is that this group consider mounting

a protest against absentee landlords, together with a program to demand enforcement of the various city building codes."

"By God!" Bob Horvath was becoming excited. "We could get them to look at that lousy elevator in my building."

The room now rang with denunciations of non-resident property owners.

". . . no heat before eight o'clock . . ."

". . . so I called up. I said this here refrigerator is twelve years old . . ."

". . . they promised . . ."

Willard Ericson had not finished. "I think a . . . er . . . public demonstration of Flensburg enthusiasm and willingness to upgrade its own community would have the happy effect of destroying whatever sympathy may have been raised by this suggestion that replacing St. Bernadette's with an apartment is going to benefit the community. I think it should be made clear that Flensburg does not need the help of outsiders."

The old fox had them in the palm of his hand, Thatcher saw. *Outsider* has always been the all-purpose epithet.

"Of course, in the meantime I shall pursue certain legal remedies to restrain this proposed sale . . ."

It is doubtful if anybody heard Ericson's last words, so skillfully had he bent the situation to his needs.

"That's the way," said a reinvigorated Bob Horvath. "Show them, show everybody that the problems here in Flensburg are our own. We can take care of them!"

Applause. Followed by further examples of evil absentee landlords. Finally:

"Say, Bob, I got a suggestion!"

"You mean you got a motion?"

"That's what we want—a motion!"

"Somebody make a motion!"

Of all people, Harry of the crossed arms rose. He glared briefly at his wife who was goggling at him. "All right, I'll make this motion. I'll make a motion that we listen to what Mr. . . . Mr. . . ."

"Ericson," said his helpmeet.

Harry gave her a look.

". . . to the lawyer. We show them that we don't need outsiders coming here to upgrade Flensburg. How's that?"

That was fine for most people. There was renewed enthusiasm. Harry sat down to the plaudits of his fellows, refolded
his arms, and exuded deep self-satisfaction. There, he seemed
to be saying to Thatcher, try to beat that!

Ericson had been studying his jury.

"That young man in the first row," he suggested in an
undertone to the chairman.

The young man rose and cleared his throat.

"Mr. Chairman. I wish to make a motion."

"Sure, sure," said Horvath. He had lost control and he
was not pretending otherwise.

Self-consciously the speaker went on: "I move that we
change the name of the St. Bernadette's Parents League to
the Flensburg Community League."

"Excellent," murmured Ericson, literally rubbing his hands
together.

"Because," said the young man, warming to his theme,
"we're not fighting for St. Bernadette School alone. We're
fighting for our entire community. You might say, our way
of life!"

There was an outburst. Harry's wife nudged Harry, then
Thatcher. The only thing missing was a brass band, playing
"The Stars and Stripes Forever."

There ensued another twenty minutes of high emotion.
Mary Foster could be heard protesting.

"But Mr. Ericson! What good will all this do us? What
is a community league going to accomplish?"

Ericson answered her only indirectly. He consulted another
piece of paper. Then, leaning over, he spoke to Horvath.

"Great, great!" said Horvath ferociously. "All right, you
out there. Quiet down! Mr. Ericson is going to tell us what
to do."

Thatcher was just as interested as everybody else in the
hall.

15

BREAD OF DECEIT

Willard Ericson's natural instinct for timing had been honed to a fine edge by years of trial experience. Like the craftsman that he was, he brought the formal meeting to a close as the surging wave of enthusiasm crested.

Excited groups milled around the large room, donning coats and hats, pledging support and assistance. The committee itself huddled over Ericson's briefcase as he displayed one paper after another. The hall rang with self-congratulation and determination.

"That's the way to go!" a dried-up little man, moving to Thatcher's side, exclaimed. "The things I could tell you about my landlord!"

"You think this is a good idea?" Thatcher asked.

The man gripped his sleeve.

"The only thing wrong with it is that it's years too late. But that's these bums for you. Make a lot of fuss about the school, they will, when they know it's wrong to go against the Cardinal. But they don't think about my rotten apartment."

Thatcher tried to unravel this tangled blend of approval and criticism.

"Then you're for the sale of the school?"

"The Cardinal knows best, doesn't he? And that apartment house will give us a boost, won't it?" The bony head bobbed forward at every question.

Thatcher was beginning to wonder how he could withdraw when deliverance appeared.

"Mr. Thatcher? Have you got a minute?"

The voice was vaguely familiar, but it took Thatcher a moment to recognize the wiry dark man.

"I'm Sal Ianello. We've already met."

Thatcher shook hands. Of course, this was the A&P manager who had routed Dick Unger.

The clutch on his arm tightened. "Hey, are you that banker? Listen, you're getting the wrong idea about Flensburg from these League people. We want that apartment house!"

Ianello took action. Over intervening heads, he called to his wife: "We're going out for some coffee, Pat. Why don't you meet us at the cafeteria? And tell Ericson, won't you?" Then he turned to the clutcher. "Sorry, Phil. We've got to run."

Within minutes, they were out on a rain-drenched street. As he turned up his collar, Ianello apologized.

"I hope you don't mind, Mr. Thatcher. Ericson said he'd be about fifteen minutes more. And I could see you wanted to get rid of Kavanaugh."

Thatcher said he was delighted to be rescued. Then memory came to his aid. "Is that the Kavanaugh you were talking about at the funeral? He seems to be a very strong supporter of Monsignor Miles."

Ianello laughed shortly as he ducked into the cafeteria on the corner. "Phil is a strong supporter of his own pocketbook. He owns that little candy store across from St. Bernadette's. When the news about the apartment house spread, he saw the chance to make a profit. He's already had one offer. He turned it down, figuring he could do better. And of course he will if the apartment house goes up."

It was clear to Thatcher. "I see. He owns his store but rents his apartment."

There was a silent nod. Sal Ianello was mulling over another problem. When he finally spoke, he had difficulty formulating his ideas.

"I didn't break in on you just because of Kavanaugh. I wanted a chance to talk to you. Look, Mr. Thatcher, you're from Wall Street. I suppose you know how these big-time lawyers operate." He paused, uncertain how to proceed. "Is Ericson always like this?"

Thatcher tried to be helpful. He explained that he had not previously known Ericson. Then he added that even the man's partners were surprised at his performance.

This innocuous statement provided Ianello with food for thought.

"So, they're surprised, too," he mused. "You know, I asked one of the company lawyers about him. He told me he's a senior partner, a specialist in fair trade. He's supposed to have a reputation for practical advice."

"Yes?" Thatcher grunted encouragingly. He could not see why this catalogue of professional achievement should be recited so glumly.

"Practical advice!" Ianello snorted. "The way he's acting, if I went to him because I was having trouble getting deliveries from the warehouse, he'd advise me to start a rival chain of supermarkets."

"You think his methods are too drastic?"

Sal did not answer the question. Instead he was suddenly inspired. "Ericson's just distributed a whole bunch of proposals. I'd like you to take a look at them."

Thatcher was not sure he wanted to supply a critical estimate of Ericson's behavior. On the other hand, he had come to Flensburg to learn what was coming. Here was an unrivaled opportunity to do so.

While Sal went off to the counter, Thatcher studied the document he had been handed. It was three pages long, and Ericson had surpassed himself. Lawsuits, mass protests and appeals to the legislature jostled for space. An unlikely array of possible allies was considered—from Mrs. Valerie Kirk through the Republican Party to the Black Panthers. Ericson might save St. Bernadette's by these tactics, but in passing he would reduce the archdiocese to a shambles, seize political control of Flensburg, oust half the property owners and put the Mass back into Latin.

"Very comprehensive," Thatcher said, at his most non-committal.

"There are a lot of things I don't know anything about," Sal admitted, savagely planting two cups of coffee on the table. "But I do know one thing. You don't get to be an expert on the fair trade laws by making like a nut!"

Thatcher reminded himself that Ianello was in the retail business. Supermarkets carried a good many fair-traded items these days.

"What exactly are you afraid of? Do you think Ericson's turning into a raving maniac?"

"I don't know exactly what I'm afraid of." Sal took a cautious sip from his cup before continuing slowly: "I'm beginning to wonder whether St. Bernadette's is what he's really aiming at. Once you get a couple of hundred people shoving around, going all out for something, you get a lot of little by-products. Hell, if you used that as a battle plan"—he flicked the typed schedule—"you'd get some pretty big ones. Ericson could have that in mind all along. Maybe that's why he's so generous with his time."

Thatcher was much more interested in listening than in speaking. Pat Ianello's arrival was a relief.

"Just coffee, Sal," she said as her husband rose. "Oh, and a cruller too."

Then she turned back to Thatcher. "What did you think of the meeting, Mr. Thatcher?" she asked earnestly.

Thatcher temporized. He wondered if she shared her husband's suspicions.

"It was not quite what I expected," he said truthfully.

"It wasn't what anybody expected. And I can't figure out what to do. Mary and I will have to get together."

"That's Mrs. Foster?"

"Yes, you see if this League is going to turn into a protest by tenants, I don't see where Mary and I come in. It's all right for Bob. He rents an apartment a couple of blocks away. But that's not true for us. Mary owns her own home. In fact, I suppose she's got two of them now that her mother's dead. And Sal and I live on the second floor of my parents' house."

"So you can't complain about absentee landlords?"

Pat was mischievous. "When we first got married, Sal would have liked them to be a little more absentee."

Thatcher did not have to be told that time had dimmed this feeling. Probably the Ianellos wouldn't be out this evening if it were not for captive baby-sitters.

"Did you and Mary decide anything?" Sal asked, returning with a tray.

"No, she's going to talk to me when she breaks free from Bob and Ericson. Bob will try to persuade her to stay." Pat wrinkled her brow in thought. "Of course, you can't blame him. Mary and I do most of the paperwork together. But she's better than I am at organizing things. Bob will really be up a creek if she resigns."

"Not to mention that he'll have to dig up the rent," Sal remarked. He explained to Thatcher. "Frank Omara was paying for our storefront out of his own pocket. We're still running on the rent he paid a couple of days before he was murdered. Mary volunteered to take over."

"I don't even know how much it is, or who it gets paid to," Pat confessed. "That's another one of our absentee land-lords. I suppose it can't cost a lot. But still the League doesn't have much money, and every little bit helps."

Sal was becoming restive. "Well, if you change direction in midstream, you have to take the consequences. The trouble with that meeting tonight is that everyone wanted something different. Even the old-timers turned out. And they blame everything on the League. Their story is that if we just eat crow and apologize to the Cathedral, everything will be normal again. We've got some hotheads of our own. They claim that the old-timers murdered Frank and are responsible for everything—from bringing in Mrs. Kirk to starting a riot. Then we've got a simple-minded bunch who want to lynch Monsignor Miles because he started the trouble by trying to sell St. Bernadette's. And," he concluded, "if we have much more of this, I'm going to start a movement to lynch Willard Ericson."

His wife's response was calm. "Everybody's always wanted different things, Sal. I mean, in the long run. We managed to sew it all together because we all wanted the same thing in the short run."

Her husband was growing philosophical.

"It's amazing how far you can go together without being bothered by wanting different things, isn't it?" He appealed to Thatcher. "But this may be the end of the line."

"You have put your finger on most popular movements," Thatcher said cautiously. "But would you explain how this applies to Flensburg?"

"It's the Parents League I'm talking about," Sal amplified. "I suppose, when you come right down to it, Bob

Horvath represents the biggest group. They're the ones who remember a world of nice little boys and girls going to parochial school and coming home to big, respectable families. They want to keep things that way. They forget that was a different world. And, for that matter, they've forgotten a lot of the nastiness in that world—like the kids who went wrong and the fathers who were drunks and wife-beaters."

Pat interrupted. "The big thing they don't remember is that everybody was held together because they were poor together. And the one thing no one has ever wanted to be is poor."

Thatcher approved. Mrs. Ianello seemed capable of recognizing economic fundamentals that escaped most practicing sociologists.

Sal ignored them both. "Then there are the people like Pat and me. We know we can't have nineteen-thirty-five, and we wouldn't have it as a gift! We're worried about the public schools, we're scared of our kids getting mixed up with drugs and violence. So in a couple of years we'll move to the suburbs. Probably the drugs and the violence will, too."

Thatcher saw an inconsistency. "Then your Parents League does seem to be representative," he said.

"No," Pat hastened to explain. "What Sal meant is that the Parents League never would have gotten off the ground if it had been left to us. The ones who really got us airborne were Frank Omara and Mary Foster. We didn't know what to do, we had no idea of how to start things. But Frank was the biggest funeral director in Flensburg. He knew almost everybody, he knew about business and how much money the Cardinal would make from selling the school. He worked up the figures about how much it cost to run the school. And he could explain it so that we all could understand."

"Yes, I can see the value of a man like that." Thatcher could also see that a man like that might have been a deterrent to Willard Ericson's planning.

"And Mary Foster worked in perfectly. She's active in every woman's group we've got. And she ran for Borough Council last election, you know. She lost, but just about everybody got to know her. And, of course, she knows all about things like local school boards and how to organize a block. It was the two of them who got the rest of us to-gether. But the funny part is that they wanted different things. It's hard to describe Frank." Pat paused, uncharac-teristically at a loss for words.

Sal tried to help. "Frank believed in ideas. For instance, he wanted something called 'Catholic education.' Myself," Sal grinned provocatively at his wife, "I think that usually turns out to be Irish education, but whatever it is, he be-lieved in it. Then, even if he was smart enough to soft-pedal it, he also wanted to take a stand for lay participation in the Church. Particularly in running the parish. He was really shocked when the archdiocese tried to railroad the sale of St. Bernadette's. You could almost say he came out like a crusader."

Thatcher tried to recall his one encounter with Francis Omara. Yes, it was possible to see the dead man as a cru-sader—a controlled and knowledgeable crusader.

"And Mrs. Foster?" he asked.

It was Pat who spoke with the authority of an expert. "Mary's a woman. She doesn't go in for the high flights. But she has a very strong sense of what's right for Flensburg. And she sticks to that, even when it's not to her advantage. Look at the way she behaved tonight. She doesn't like this campaign about absentee landlords. She says it will take attention away from St. Bernadette's. And I think she's right." Pat was very sober. "And you have to admire her. She could make an election issue out of these landlords. Sometimes I think she's too uncompromising. She didn't even want Sal and me to look at Mr. Unger's project over on Staten Island. I know Mr. Unger isn't going to come over to our side, but I don't think it does any harm to talk to him."

"I don't think it did," Thatcher agreed.

"But I don't want you to think Mary isn't a realist. She's ready to fight for St. Bernadette's. I heard her laying it on the line to Father James when he criticized her for starting the Parents League."

"Father James." Thatcher was roused by the name. "He has been a consistent opponent of the Parents League, hasn't he?"

Pat smiled broadly. "He's a consistent critic of everybody.

He thinks he's a liberal, but he wants to ram through his ideas like an old-fashioned parish priest. He tried to lecture me about Christian marriage."

"Well, if they do away with celibacy and he gets himself a wife," Sal said lazily, "that's the last we'll hear about that."

Pat was immediately lost in speculation. Who had the potential, she asked, to make the wife that Father James deserved? "There's Sharon Farrell," she answered happily. "That girl is going to turn into a real henpecker, I can see it coming."

The conversation might well have protracted itself beyond Thatcher's competence had it not been for the arrival of Mary Foster. She got right down to business.

"Things aren't as bad as you think, Pat," she said, hanging up a damp raincoat. "But someone is going to have to talk sense to them sooner or later." She paused to look at Thatcher thoughtfully. "I don't suppose you . . . ?"

Thatcher hastily declared himself not responsible for Willard Ericson.

"I didn't really think so," Mary sighed. "I suppose it's up to us. Bob will listen to reason once he's cooled down. He'll see this won't do any good. And, Mr. Thatcher, I do realize that you've already done a lot for us. If nobody else has thanked you for taking enough interest to come out here tonight, I'd like to."

"I enjoyed it," said Thatcher. Surprisingly, this was so.

"Mr. Ericson asked me to tell you that he's finished. He's waiting for you across the street." Her teeth glinted in a sudden smile. "I guess he didn't think he'd be very popular over here. He knows how Pat and I feel."

It would, Thatcher reflected, take someone made of solid oak not to know. Sal Ianello followed him to the door.

"You won't forget what I said about Ericson, will you?" he said, reverting to their earlier conversation.

"No," Thatcher promised.

But Ianello had more to say. "I'd give a lot to know what Frank Omara said in his last talk with Monsignor Miles, wouldn't you?"

Thatcher was startled. Had the trend of Ianello's suspicions changed?

"Why?" he asked baldly.

Sal was almost too ingenuous. "Frank was upset during that last meeting. He wasn't cheerful the way he usually was. He had something on his mind all right. And if that was why he was murdered, it was probably still on his mind the next evening. Monsignor Miles was the logical person for him to talk to. And I can't help remembering one thing. I can still hear what Frank said at the meeting. He was surprised someone was trying to exploit St. Bernadette's. I think he meant someone was trying to make money out of it, don't you?"

As he stepped over the flooded gutter, Thatcher realized how shrewdly Ianello had made his last point. Very few bankers could have failed to agree with him.

16

THE CHIEF PLACE OF CONCOURSE

The events of the following Thursday were due almost entirely to an unfortunate mischance. The owner of Bob Horvath's building, Mr. Sirius Meeks, himself resided in an apartment on United Nations Plaza.

This fact had not been previously known in Flensburg. There, the owner was known as Blue Hill Realty, Incorporated, and emerged in the form of an impersonal rent collector. But once Willard Ericson turned his mind to the problem of absentee landlords, it was the work of minutes to tear aside the veil of corporate anonymity. It did not take much longer to rouse local enthusiasm for a demonstration in Mr. Meeks's backyard. Indeed, the magnitude of the response was surprising. People who were too young to have children, people who were too old to have children, and people who were already sending children to public school, all flocked to the St. Bernadette's Parents League in its new guise.

The membership of the Action Committee was still unchanged, in spite of Pat Ianello's reluctance.

"Don't you think we should resign, Mary?" she had asked. "No matter what Bob says, you didn't start the League to take on absentee landlords."

"No, I don't think we should," Mary had replied vigorously. "Somebody has to stay here and fight for St. Bernadette's. I don't exactly know how. But if that Ericson man can produce one miracle, maybe he can come up with another one."

"I don't think he's very interested in St. Bernadette's now," Pat replied crossly.

"The only one who knows what that old goat is interested in is Willard Ericson himself!"

And so, with mixed emotions, the Action Committee determined to march at the head of its followers. Thanks to the New York subway system—often maligned, often threatened, but somehow still functioning—three hundred protesters were able to make the trip from Flensburg and to parade into United Nations Plaza.

Their arrival astonished the New York City police.

Let any situation become repetitive enough and those in charge become victims of a single fixed idea. Thus, for over eighteen months, the same orders had been issued to the men guarding the United Nations. *Whatever else happens, keep a clear space of fifty yards between the Jewish pickets and the Arab pickets!* Splendid as this strategy was, it made no allowance for the advent of a third faction.

"Who the hell are they?" asked one startled patrolman.

"They've got signs," his partner observed.

The signs were not designed to be helpful. They were the result of individual zeal.

CATHOLIC CHURCHMEN UNITE!

DOWN WITH MEEKS!

ST. BERNADETTE'S FOR BETTER LIVING

FRANCIS OMARA DID NOT DIE IN VAIN!

FLENSBURG MARCHES FORWARD

"Who's Meeks?" the dazed patrolman demanded.

"Who's Omara?"

"Maybe he was killed in the Sinai," the first one said dubiously. It did not sound likely, even to his own ears.

But his partner was already busy at the two-way radio.

"Tell the commissioner the Catholics have come!" he blurted out.

At Headquarters there was justifiable bewilderment.

"Do you mean that now *we* want Jerusalem?" exclaimed a deputy commissioner.

The commissioner's onerous responsibilities encouraged brutal realism.

"If we do," he rejoined, "this is a bad time to try and get it."

Enlightenment might never have dawned if the police had been left to talk exclusively with each other. But other voices were soon raised. The belligerents already entrenched in United Nations Plaza were not men to suffer in silence. First there was loud disbelief. Then there was polyglot grievance at trespass. Finally, there was the first common ground in many a year. Jew and Arab alike started a nasty seepage toward the newcomers. The police intervened; spokesmen were appointed and advanced under a flag of truce. General clarification prevailed.

"Too much clarification, if you ask me, sir," announced the lieutenant who had taken over communications. "The Jews and the Arabs say they have rotten landlords, too. In fact, one of the Jordanians was telling me you wouldn't believe the housing conditions over in Crown Heights."

"Forget Crown Heights!" barked the radio. "What I want to know is whether everything is peaceful in the Plaza."

"Oh, everybody's getting along like a house afire. But, sir, what do you want me to do about permits for this new bunch?"

"So long as they're not giving any trouble, forget about permits. We've got important things to worry about."

Possibly Headquarters misread the situation. Possibly, too, Headquarters was not disposed to lavish manpower on slum landlords living in penthouses. In either case, Mr. Sirius Meeks was not swaddled with police protection.

Subsequent developments came as no surprise to the lieutenant.

It was a clear, bright and bitterly cold day. Gusts from the East River ripped through the open Plaza with knife-edged velocity. The old pros were outfitted for Arctic conditions. As suffering threatened the Flensburg contingent, Jews and Arabs rallied around with aids to survival. First came the offer of earmuffs and wool gloves for the stricken. Then advice about handling large placards so they did not turn into mighty wind-filled mainsails. Finally, eleven o'clock signaled an elaborate coffee break. This was not the end of the contest. Delicacy vied with delicacy.

"What do they call this stuff with the sesame seeds?" Bob Horvath asked as he nuzzled an oily handful.

Pat Ianello was too busy to answer. She was trying to extract the recipe for her chopped liver sandwich from a motherly woman.

And amidst apricot paste and cold *flanken*, everyone swapped atrocity stories about landlords. The accents differed, the details were the same—elevators out of service for months, inadequate heat, rampant vermin. Not surprisingly, when replacements arrived to picket the United Nations, the shifts going off duty lingered to support their new-found friends.

"Sooner or later," the lieutenant predicted, "some reporter is going to realize this is a story."

He was strolling through the assorted groups like a proud kindergarten teacher approving the behavior of his charges. Everything, he reported hourly, was going just fine.

If the lieutenant had paused to think, he would have recalled that there is one group even more sensitive to the publicity value of current events than the press. That group is composed of men who run for elective office. And United Nations Plaza is home to quite a large number of them. As word of the presence of anti-Meeks forces percolated into the byways of Manhattan, the phone calls started.

"Listen, Amanda, this is serious," said young Carlton Briggs; "I don't know when I'll be home."

Amanda dropped the chain of turquoise beads she had been considering to give the phone her undivided attention.

"What do you mean, you don't know when you'll be home? Have you forgotten that we have over a hundred guests arriving at five o'clock?"

"I know that. But I can't come back as long as those pickets are in front of the building. Are they still there?" Mr. Briggs sounded hysterical.

Amanda's interests in life were restricted, but they included society page coverage of her parties. She drifted to the window, looked out dutifully, and reported back.

"They're still there, honey, but what do they have to do with us? I passed them this morning. They're some kind of Catholic group."

"Amanda, they're picketing a slum landlord who lives in our building. And I'm running for city council! I can't afford to get involved!"

"Carlton, I'm not asking you to get involved," Amanda said with heavy patience; "I'm just asking you to come home. How can I have a party without you?"

"What if somebody stops me? What if some reporter asks me to give my views? What if he asks me how I like having a slum landlord for a neighbor? I'm running on the Democratic ticket," young Briggs reminded his wife, who tended to forget. "That's hard enough when you're rich."

Unfortunately Amanda's vagrant attention had been caught by one phrase. "Well, Carlton, why *do* we have a slum landlord for a neighbor?"

"Because he can afford to live at UN Plaza," her husband snarled. "Now, honey, I want you to promise me you'll stay inside. I don't want them catching you, either. With luck, nobody will realize we live there."

The chief occupation of Amanda Briggs's life was letting people know where she lived. She decided that, for some reason, this was turning into one of those occasions on which men are difficult.

"No, Carlton," she said sweetly, "I won't go out. I'll be too busy getting ready for the party. And, remember, I always said we should live in the Dakota!"

Every politician in the building made a call virtually identical to this one. At the same time, Police Headquarters went momentarily insane when its information retrieval system reported that Mr. Sirius Meeks had Anglicized his name some thirty years ago upon emigrating from Beirut.

"Don't let anyone know!" they ordered the lieutenant.

Father James was also making telephone calls. He had been detailed to join the Flensburg protest by Father Doyle out of a variety of motives. First, of course, anything that got Father James out of Queens and simultaneously slaked his thirst for social movements was a good thing. Second, Monsignor Miles's remarks about confining the conflagration to Flensburg had rankled at the time and they still rankled. When Father James's third call reported that television crews had finally arrived, a small thin smile spread over Father Doyle's face.

In the midst of all this calling, sooner or later a new number was going to occur to some of the participants. That was what Willard Ericson had had in mind all along. At approximately four-thirty, the calls to husbands, wives, policemen and ecclesiastical superiors stopped.

Everyone started calling Mr. Sirius Meeks.

"My own neighbors turning against me!" he lamented.

His wife, who had been running the blockade while he skulked inside, said that it was becoming a major inconvenience for the whole building.

"They're not used to inconveniences," she pointed out.

"And how did they make their money?" Mr. Meeks inquired sardonically over the shrilling of the telephone bell. "If the truth were known, it— Oh, never mind, I'll get it."

This time it was some unknown Catholic priest. "He wanted to talk to me about my responsibilities to his flock!" Mr. Meeks thundered.

"If he can't talk to you, he'll talk to television," said Mrs. Meeks. She did not know how right she was.

Father James did talk to television. So did Bob Horvath, Sidney Ginsberg and Ahmed Abdullah. Only forcible detention kept Phil Kavanaugh from advancing on the microphones.

"Think of the terrible impression he'd make," Pat Ianello gasped in the ensuing scuffle.

Those who did speak made a splendid impression. The commissioner himself said so when he finally sped to the scene. "Everybody is using a lot of restraint," he said, ignoring a spirited debate occurring just out of camera range. He shivered in the icy blast from the East River. "It's heartwarming to see New Yorkers conducting an orderly protest like this. I'm proud of them, and I'm proud of the police. It's been a long hard day for all of us, but it's a day we can all be . . . um . . . proud of."

He triggered an orgy of self-congratulation. Mr. Richard J. Dumbleby, vice president of CBS and manager of station WCBS entitled his editorial "The Great People of a Great City."

". . . factionalism, group pitted against group," he read carefully. "But what did we see at United Nations Plaza today? We saw Jews and Arabs joining their Catholic brethren, submerging differences for the common good. Perhaps we can all learn a lesson from the men and women of Flensburg—the lesson that there is at least as much binding us together as dividing us . . ."

Every editor, columnist, minister and politician in the city recognized a Heaven-sent text. Here, in a world of tragedy and anguish, there is goodness, there is hope, there is brotherhood.

Even in New York.

It was a terrible week for Mr. Sirius Meeks.

17

BE THOU DILIGENT

The Police Commissioner and the networks might glow with tempered approval. Bob Horvath was frankly jubilant.

"Did you see what Channel Eleven called us?" he asked happily. "A community fighting to save itself! How about that?"

Horvath was leading a victory celebration. The general

intoxication of seeing Flensburg right up there with Washington, Saigon, and Peking had filled headquarters to overflowing. The party was in full swing.

"Did you see that cartoon in the *Daily News?*"

"My son in Omaha—he called up last night. They showed us on TV out there. Would you believe it?"

But new enthusiasms had not submerged old memories.

"We sure showed them, huh, Bob?" demanded a follower. "Frank would have been proud of us."

Horvath put down his can of beer and spoke earnestly: "We're going to do a lot more for Frank's memory. If it wasn't for him, we wouldn't be here today." He grew almost evangelical. "We haven't begun to fight yet. Meeks is only the start. They won't recognize Flensburg once we're through. We'll go after every single one of those stinking landlords."

There was a roar of applause over lifted beer cans.

"Now we've got the clout, we'll use it. We're not gonna let anybody push us around anymore!"

Ruthie nearly burst with pride. She had been right all along. Stepping into Frank's shoes had made a new man out of Bob. . . .

At the Chancery, Henry Stronor was not jubilant. He was, however, cautiously optimistic. After prolonged thought, he had concluded that United Nations Plaza would promote, not retard, Church interests.

His reasoning was persuasive. "In the first place, the whole demonstration by these Flensburg parents had nothing to do with religious matters. They were protesting absentee landlords . . ."

A casual question from Father Livingston reinforced Henry's conviction.

"No. Mr. Meeks is secular, if anything ever was. Then, too, this entire uproar happened a long way from St. Bernadette's. The television crews were in the Plaza. The cameras showed pickets at the United Nations. Reporters were interviewing Manhattan politicians. Anybody in public relations will tell you that the school has become a dead issue."

"But . . ."

"Finally," Henry said triumphantly, "remember how peaceful and orderly the protest was. There was nothing to make a scandal for us. No overturned cars. No arrests."

Father Livingston was silent. After the Bhagavad Catholics, the Chancery was ready to be grateful for almost anything.

"As we see it," Henry summarized, already visualizing the words in typeset, "this new program of the Parents League has improved the outlook for a rational, correct solution to the vexed problem of selling St. Bernadette's."

There was no argument from Father Livingston. Henry rose, squared his slight shoulders, and prepared to put his case before Monsignor Miles. For once, he thought without arrogance, there were no flaws in his logic. Monsignor Miles must agree that there was no impediment to optimism.

It is always harder to convert a man to pessimism than to optimism. Mary Foster was beginning to fear that the task might be beyond her powers.

"Mr. Ericson," she insisted, "I still don't see where all this is going to lead."

In his hour of triumph, Willard Ericson could afford to be generous.

"I'm sorry if I haven't made it clear, Mrs. Foster. We have already made considerable progress. The television coverage alone has been an extraordinary asset. Of course, we were fortunate to become a human interest story. Those pickets at the United Nations . . ."

Mary was less patient with Ericson's prolixity than she had been.

"I know about the television coverage," she broke in without apology. "I know everybody is patting us on the back. That's not what I mean by getting somewhere. People in Flensburg are interested in two things. Most of us want to save St. Bernadette's. Some of us want landlord complaints taken care of."

Ericson could interrupt, too. He looked at her over his glasses.

"You are not yourself a tenant, I understand?" he asked dispassionately.

Color was beginning to flush Mary's cheeks.

"No, I'm not! Everybody knows that. But I can still

understand people's complaints about heating and hot water. I am willing to work to help them. Only, the way to help them is to enforce the building code, not make fools of ourselves in UN Plaza! I admit we've given Mr. Meeks a bad time. But that isn't the same as getting heat and hot water!"

Ericson had deliberately roused Mary; now he used her response.

"I am afraid"—he shook his head sadly—"that you are exaggerating. Of course Mr. Horvath and the tenants want a practical solution for their difficulties. Just as you want to save the school. But you agreed to ask for an injunction against the Unger sale, didn't you?"

"Because it would stop the sale, that's why!" she snapped.

"No, Mrs. Foster, I must correct you. The suit was filed to bring pressure on the archdiocese. And, ultimately, that is precisely what these tenant protests will do as well. If sufficient public sympathy is roused for Flensburg, the archdiocese will be in danger of being confused with slum landlords."

Mary sighed, defeated.

"I wonder," she said, "if Monsignor Miles sees things that way."

"Let us hope not, Mrs. Foster." Ericson smiled diabolically. "Let us hope he does not see it until too late."

For once, Father Doyle and Father James were in accord on a controversial issue. United Nations Plaza, they agreed, was a blessing.

That, unfortunately, was the beginning and the end of harmony. From there they proceeded rapidly in opposite directions.

"One thing I'll say," said Father Doyle mellowly, allowing himself an after-dinner cigar. "We have a united parish here in Flensburg once again. These have always been good people and faithful ones. I've told the Cathedral that, time and time again. As for carryings-on over in Manhattan . . ." He waved them away in a cloud of smoke.

Father James, who admired asceticism, had quivered at the cigar. Now he quivered further.

This was not lost on his superior.

"I saw you on television," Father Doyle said indulgently. "There won't be need for much more of that, will there?"

He spoke with avuncular affection. United Nations Plaza was a blessing, Father Doyle had said, and he meant it. He did not intend to throw it away.

"Now, with our people busying themselves elsewhere," he said, inspecting his ash narrowly, "I think we can all go back to what we were. If Robert Horvath and his friends wish to bedevil their landlords—well, I say more power to them! We here at St. Bernadette's can take up our priestly duties— and forget these bad times."

Father James was passionate. "Can we forget about murder?"

With an effort, Father Doyle kept his temper. "No, my boy, we cannot forget murder or any other mortal sin. But we remember them in the sanctuary and the confessional."

Father James, too, had made several good resolutions.

"Father Doyle," he said, "we cannot lock ourselves in the church. We must involve ourselves—the Church must involve itself—in the concerns of our parishioners. United Nations Plaza may be in Manhattan—but it is vital to Flensburg."

Father Doyle's thickened fingers began a slow tattoo on the polished dining-room table.

"Without a social conscience," Father James continued beseechingly, "the Church will perish."

Father Doyle eyed him. "Now understand me, Father! I meant what I said. There is to be no more of this nonsense —from you. Discharge your obligations. You have many. Visit the sick, comfort the weary, guide the young!"

The mulish cast of Father James's jaw goaded him further: "And stay off television!"

Father James took a deep breath.

"Father, much as I respect and love you, I must question your decision. Flensburg is at the center of one of the most dramatic confrontations of our time. We have it in our power to prove that the Church can help Catholics in their daily life. That we are not just providing Mass on Sunday and ignoring the rest of the week. The Flensburg Community League—"

"STOP!" It was the familiar voice of thunder. "I will hear no more. The Flensburg Community League! Father James, community leagues have no need of priests! And priests have no need of community leagues! Now"—he aimed his cigar like a pistol—"now let there be an end to this. Let us—for God's sake—have peace!"

18

PERVERSE IN HIS WAYS

After that historic assault on the domestic comfort of Sirius Meeks, John Putnam Thatcher read one editorial, watched one television program, and received, at second hand, the views of Charlie Trinkam's Catherine. It was enough, he felt, to make him master of the situation. Recalling Willard Ericson's give-'em-hell tactics and Sal Ianello's growing distrust, he knew that elation, relief, and misgiving must be among the emotions provoked by this latest antic of Flensburg's embattled citizenry.

It never occurred to him that—in one quarter, at least—the foray into United Nations Plaza was being hailed as confirmation of strong suspicions. Not until the two men were seated across his desk did he realize that he was in danger of becoming an expert witness.

The police opened the interview disarmingly.

"I guess you didn't expect to see us back here, Mr. Thatcher."

Thatcher replied that as long as Francis Omara's murder remained unsolved, he welcomed signs of police activity. What could he do for them?

"We're still interested in that meeting the day before murder."

They took him through his only encounter with Omara.

Then they went a step further and asked for details about the birth of the tenants' crusade.

Finally the clincher came.

"It's like this, Mr. Thatcher. Nobody really doubts that Omara was killed because he was heading the Parents League. But, if that's true, then you'd expect his death to make some difference to the League. Otherwise, why bother to kill him?"

Thatcher was beginning to see where this road led.

"At the time of the funeral," he offered, "there were people who thought the League might stop obstructing the sale of St. Bernadette's with Omara gone."

This neutral trial balloon was instantly shot down.

"The committee didn't stop." For the lieutenant, facts were facts. "From what I hear, the League was never in any doubt about going on. No, that wasn't the change the murderer hoped for. At headquarters, we've been waiting. And look what's happened! As soon as the funeral is decently over, as soon as that birth control riot throws up a smoke screen, the League turns in its tracks, forgets all about the school, and goes chasing off after absentee landlords. Do you think that would have happened if Francis Omara was still running the show?"

Thatcher made all the normal protestations. He had met Omara only once. The surviving members of the Committee were virtual strangers.

"But your impressions, Mr. Thatcher?"

The police wanted an answer and, unfortunately, there was one.

"It was my impression that Omara and Mrs. Foster together could run the League the way they wanted," Thatcher said honestly.

"And now?"

Thatcher could only report that Mrs. Foster did not seem happy with the new look, but her influence was not what it had been.

"I think there was some question of Mrs. Foster and Mrs. Ianello resigning."

The detectives were settling down.

"The way we see it," said the elder cozily, "this tenant protest was railroaded through by Ericson. But Horvath was right there, ready to jump on the bandwagon. He could have set the whole thing up beforehand. He's the chairman, he's the one who's talking to the lawyer."

Involuntarily Thatcher remembered Horvath's descent on the Sloan. He had been fresh from a conference with Willard Ericson. And, in his own way, he had warned Thatcher that the Parents League might be setting a new course. Had he been referring to a plot already laid?

Thatcher was happy to say he knew nothing about the origins of the tenants' crusade. On their subway ride to Flensburg, Ericson had promised to spring a new issue. He had not elaborated further.

"You're a banker, Mr. Thatcher," the lieutenant said incontestably. "How does it look to you? Omara claims someone is trying to use the League. He's killed the next day. Then, by God, the League is used to attack property owners. The attacks won't stop, you know. Horvath wants to go after all the absentee landlords. Would it surprise the hell out of you if a lot of owners decided to unload?"

As a banker, Thatcher had to agree that there was something in what the lieutenant said.

"I thought you'd see it that way." The detectives looked at each other. They were not congratulating themselves. They were preparing the next step. "We've told Meeks we want to know about the first offer he gets. But that may take time. We'd like any shortcuts we can find."

Thatcher knew his duty. He reminded his visitors that Francis Omara had been a troubled man when he spoke with Monsignor Miles, only hours before his murder.

"If anyone can provide a shortcut, it will be the Monsignor."

The detective nodded quietly. "Good. I was hoping you'd say that. You and Monsignor Miles are the real outsiders in this deal. If we get a break, it's probably going to come from one of you two."

The lieutenant rose. "Our next stop is the Cathedral. But I hope you'll go on thinking about this. You might remember something."

"I shall certainly do my best," Thatcher promised.

But no one was more surprised than he an hour later. He was dictating a letter.

". . . do not forsee any substantial decline in our prime rate of interest. In spite of the action of the Worcester County Bank . . ."

The silence became too protracted for Miss Corsa.

"Mr. Thatcher?" she said, reproach in every syllable.

"What? . . . Oh, I beg your pardon, Miss Corsa. But I have just remembered something that Ianello mentioned. That man Kavanaugh received an offer for his candy store. It would be interesting to know when."

There was yet another reaction to United Nations Plaza that would come as a surprise to John Thatcher.

It began with a telephone call from an expensive hideaway in the Caribbean.

"Dick? Is that you, Dick?" the voice asked irascibly.

"I'll have Mr. Unger on the line in a moment," trilled the switchboard operator.

Dick Unger, arriving posthaste from the men's room, picked up the receiver in time to overhear a familiar aside.

"I don't know what the hell's wrong with that boy, Doris. He can't handle clients, he can't handle the press, and now he's not even there to answer the phone!"

"Hullo, Dad," said Dick Unger with an automatic lurch in the pit of his stomach.

"Oh, there you are!" It was an accusation.

"I was just down the hall."

Unger senior snorted. "I wish you'd stop wasting time and do something about this Flensburg mess!"

"Do what?" Dick bleated. "Is it my fault that things have turned out this way?"

"You don't seem to be helping any. What are you planning to do? Just give up, after we've gone this far?"

"Dad, I don't think you realize what we've got on our hands. This is turning into a real catastrophe."

"You know," his father told him with sinister calm, "we get the papers down here."

"I know you do!" As far as Dick was concerned, this was no advantage. "Did you read about that demonstration in UN Plaza? What do you expect me to do? Break it up with wrecking balls?"

He could now be heard three offices down the corridor. Sooner or later this moment arrived during every Unger family call.

"Listen, pinhead, don't ask me what I've read! I'm asking you what Unger Realty is going to say."

"What can we say?" Dick growled.

"Christ! What have I done to deserve this?" Unger senior asked passionately.

"But, Dad"—it was almost a howl—"the demonstrators want to keep the community unchanged—except for fixing things up. We want to tear down their school and build an apartment house. Logically we can't be on the same side. So what can we say?"

There was a long silence. When Unger next spoke, he was beholding a natural wonder.

"Logic I get! Do I need logic? Listen, those guys in the Plaza with signs—they're against slum housing. Right? Well, for Crissake! Are we *for* slum housing? Have you ever noticed the kind of building Unger Realty puts up?"

Dick had screwed his eyes shut. At every explosive demand he nodded or shook his head, as the case required.

"All right, Dad, all right," he muttered. "We're against slum housing."

"And what was their other big point? Oh, yeah—they're opposed to outside interference. Well, you call in the reporters and you make a big statement. Unger Realty is joining the parade. We're against slum housing and outside interference, too!"

"But, Dad!" Dick summoned energy for one last protest. "By outside interference they mean us."

"Well," his father retorted combustively, "by outside interference, I mean the government. But you don't have to tell them that, do you?"

Resistance crumbled.

"Okay, okay. I'll do it today."

"And make it strong while you're at it! That's all—what, Doris? Oh, your mother wants to talk to you."

Mrs. Unger should have been an improvement. Unfortunately she wanted to discuss her grandchildren, thereby deflecting her son's thoughts into a disastrous preview of the future. Dick Unger could see himself, in a few short years, sandwiched between two generations, both critical and, on occasion, openly hostile.

However, he had work to do.

"Lily," he told the intercom, after speeding his parents back to the beach, "you'd better come in. I've got a press release to dictate . . ."

Thus, within twenty-four hours, an essentially vacuous statement about Flensburg became available to the reading public. This, in turn, sparked competition.

"Good God!" said a man on the third floor of the Sloan Guaranty Trust. "Look at this! We can't afford to be the only ones who aren't supporting the Parents League. We've got to say something . . ."

Soon, another press release had been composed. Not surprisingly, this one emphasized the Sloan's distaste for substandard housing, absentee landlords and defective plumbing. The Sloan, it proclaimed, stood foursquare behind the efforts of Flensburg—or indeed any American community—to improve the quality of life.

Of necessity, press releases from banks cannot deal exclusively with moral platitudes. Frequently a number must be mentioned. For this reason, the Sloan Public Relations Department was required to secure approval from a responsible officer for its creations. As the third floor saw this, it was the eternal conflict between Art and Mammon.

"I thought, Thatcher, that you would be interested in seeing our release on the Unger-St. Bernadette's situation." The PR Director was impersonating a man who just happened to be passing when struck by this idea.

"Thank you." Thatcher never insisted on ramming unpalatable facts down subordinate throats without necessity.

He read with interest that the Sloan, inspired by the highest civic ideals, was holding in abeyance any decision on the Unger mortgage funds until the situation had *clarified to the satisfaction of local residents.*

Renshaw was visibly pained as Thatcher reached for a pencil.

"We checked with your secretary about the Bank's policy," he said.

"You've got the policy right," Thatcher said cheerfully. "Just a few minor changes. I'm afraid we'll have to take out anything that suggests a specific period of time. And I don't like this reference to the satisfaction of local residents. Some of them are going to be dissatisfied no matter what happens. We'd better make that *until the situation with respect to local residents has been clarified.*"

Renshaw knew better than to criticize Thatcher's prose. He did, however, feel he had an important contribution to make.

"I thought a time period, in general terms at least, would be desirable. There is much interest in the financial community about how long these funds will be tied up." He caught the frown on Thatcher's face and explained further. "That's because money is tight now."

For the first time Thatcher looked up and closely examined the man across the desk. He disliked dealing with the Public Relations Department and avoided doing so whenever possible. Due to the success of this policy, and the rapid turnover in the department, he rarely saw the same PR man twice. Why, then, he wondered, was he afflicted with this sense of *déjà vu?*

Ah! Suddenly he remembered. It was from that very same chair, a scant six months ago, that Renshaw's predecessor had carefully explained to him that when interest rates go up, the price of bonds goes down. Thatcher did not object to the Sloan's educating the PR men caught in its revolving doors. If only they did not all become so generous with their newly acquired knowledge.

"There," he said, laying down his pencil, "that will do."

By rights, the paragraph should have appeared in modest obscurity on the financial page. But the New York papers, still enamored of the Arab-Israeli Entente, were giving its consequences inflated coverage. The Sloan paragraph, much expanded, appeared on front pages. Depending on editorial policy, it was heralded as proof of private industry's sensitivity to the problems of our time or, alternatively, of the power of the people to seize the initiative and bend the Establishment to its will.

Neither interpretation impressed Thatcher. But as he read the stories, he was satisfied. Thanks to his modifications, the Sloan's statement was entirely meaningless.

"Now that," he said to himself, "can't do any harm!"

Rarely had he been so mistaken.

19

RICHES ARE NOT FOREVER

It took very little time for the Sloan's bromides about better housing to drive someone to unexpected lengths. Thatcher's first intimation of impending tumult came with his arrival in the office next morning. Miss Corsa, in the outer room, was staring at a letter in some perplexity.

In itself, this was bad. Miss Corsa did not regard it as one of her duties to be perturbed by the contents of the mail. Her job was to separate the urgent from the routine, to supply any files or backup material required for an answer, and, finally, to nag Mr. Thatcher into taking care of tiresome letters that had been left pending too long. If the correspondence brought bad news, if it called for agonizing decisions, if it made unreasonable demands on the Sloan Guaranty Trust—well, senior vice presidents are paid substantial salaries to cope with that kind of problem.

But worse was to come. Miss Corsa had raised her eyes and was considering him appraisingly. One finger hovered briefly over the telephone dial. Then she changed her mind.

"Perhaps," she said in a very slow and careful voice, "perhaps you had better see this, Mr. Thatcher."

Simmering, he stretched out a hand. John Thatcher knew perfectly well that there were many things his secretary did not tell him. She did not regard him as a suitable confidant for her gleanings from the Sloan grapevine. And who could say she was wrong? But when it came to censoring his correspondence, she was going too far. Thatcher had half formed a denunciation when his peripheral vision stopped him cold.

He was not holding the customary typed business communication. He was holding a sheet of paper onto which small pieces of newsprint had been pasted to form a message. It was short.

DOWN WITH ALL ENEMIES OF ST. BERNADETTE'S!
A BOMB WILL GO OFF IN THIS BUILDING TODAY.

Wordlessly, Thatcher turned to the envelope now being extended to him. Primitive printing said simply:

JOHN THATCHER
SIXTH FLOOR

At last he looked up and met Miss Corsa's eyes. Matching her own control, he said gravely, "Very interesting."

Then he broke off and shook his head irately. No, this would not do! He was allowing himself to be mesmerized by Miss Corsa. Left to their own devices, the two of them could continue demonstrating their immunity to panic until the building blew up.

"It is not interesting!" he bellowed. "It is outrageous!" Then, for good measure, he slammed his fist on her desk.

A woman who is not stampeded by a time bomb is not going to be impressed by a show of force.

"What would you like me to do?" she inquired with icy composure.

"Get me the police!" he thundered, stalking into his own office.

But once he was connected with Centre Street, he was curiously embarrassed. Melodrama had never been his forte.

"New York City Police Headquarters," a voice announced.

"This is the senior vice president of the Sloan Guaranty Trust," Thatcher began. Then, in funereal tempo, he continued: "We have just received a letter claiming there is a bomb on the premises."

This was a familiar refrain at Centre Street.

"You want the bomb squad," the voice said kindly.

During the inevitable clicks and buzzes, Thatcher had time to meditate on the state of a society where calls like his were commonplace.

"Hello!" the receiver boomed. "This is Captain Rasche. I hear you've got a bomb letter. Just give me the name and address, will you?"

Captain Rasche was a specialist. There was nothing to it, according to him. They would evacuate all personnel, they would search the building, defusing as they went. It would be business as usual within three or four hours.

"This is a rather large building," Thatcher warned.

"So were Macy's and Rockefeller Center," the Captain reminded him. "I'll just coordinate with our Bank Department. We'll have a team there in fifteen minutes. It's a lucky thing you're so handy."

In spite of these reassurances, Thatcher still thought that evacuating the Sloan might prove more complicated than the Captain realized. He was right.

At the emergency meeting which he summoned, the director of bank security was the first to speak up.

"I don't believe in this bomb for a minute," he said flatly.

"You mean it's just a hoax?" Charlie Trinkam was frankly disappointed. For the first time in years, his working day promised more entertainment than his extracurricular life.

"Hoax, hell! This is the first step in a bank robbery. Do you realize that all the time locks are open during banking hours?"

The police, rather to Thatcher's surprise, did not dismiss this idea.

"Our bank boys thought of that one themselves," Captain Rasche said, on arriving with a large supporting cast. "So we've got a plan."

The plan, it developed, consisted of surrounding the bank with an impressive cordon of armed police. The evacuees would be passed through the cordon, which would remain in place—facing outwards—until the search was complete.

"Nothing short of an army will be able to fight its way through," Rasche promised hoarsely.

The next objection came from the bank auditors. No one, they said darkly, absolutely no one could be allowed into

the vaults in the absence of the examiners. That included
New York City policemen.

"Very well," Thatcher said resignedly. "We will evacuate
the building and search the office floors. By that time, we
should have representatives of the auditors and the state
examiners on hand. Then we can do the vaults."

But even the evacuation presented its own problems. All
employees were urged to march promptly out of the building.
The first six floors would use the stairs, the remainder would
use the elevators.

Only half of those on the payroll chose to honor these
directions. An embellishment was soon added to the original
instructions. Someone suggested that the fugitives sing (and
everybody suspected the head of the Glee Club, a man who
did not find much artistic release in the computer section).
Thatcher was not averse to any attempt to keep the retreat
orderly. He did, however, deprecate the choice of *Nearer My
God to Thee*. In the first place, it was anticlimactic: the
employees were not going down with the *Titanic*. Secondly,
many marchers seemed unfamiliar with the hymn. And thirdly,
those who knew the hymn were incapable of singing it correctly.

But Everett Gabler, who approved all disciplined per-
formances, exclaimed from his vantage point on the balcony:
"It's an impressive sight, isn't it?"

"If you care for that sort of thing," Thatcher replied
austerely.

The early departers were willing to flee empty-handed.
Not so the loiterers. They appeared, eventually, bearing with
them precious belongings. The Law Department, to a man,
had chosen to bring along its files. Once free of the building,
they set down their manila folders and squatted in a pro-
tective circle within the larger protection of the police cordon.

"There are lots of people," the general counsel hissed,
"who'd give their eye teeth to see these files."

In view of the fact that the Sloan was currently cooperating with investigations by the Federal Trade Commission, the
Department of Justice, the Currency Committee of the House
of Representatives and the New York State Banking Commission, Thatcher could only regard these precautions as

ludicrous. Unless, of course, there was more in those files than he knew.

The Real Estate Department had been equally assiduous. After commandeering an elevator for their exclusive use, they had brought down one trolley after another filled with brown cardboard boxes. They were now encamped around a towering pile which must include every mortgage held by the Sloan. From the looks they were darting southward, they expected a raid by the Law Department.

"Remarkable!" murmured Charlie Trinkam, who was strolling happily about, his hands in his pockets.

Thatcher wondered where those cardboard boxes came from. Did Real Estate live in perpetual readiness for flight? He reminded himself to take a closer look at their operations when he had more leisure.

Many of the staff clutched personal possessions. George Lancer's secretary, in his absence, had ostentatiously borne to safety the silver-framed photograph of his wife. Thatcher considered this objectively. George, he knew, was devoted to Lucy. But George was a realist. So long as he had the original, he was not likely to overvalue a Bachrach portrait. There was only one explanation. Miss Evans was trying to go beyond the call of duty.

His own Miss Corsa had her little tin box. That box lived in the bottom drawer of her desk and had been an enduring challenge to Thatcher's imagination. Normally it was undisturbed. But at intervals Miss Corsa would remove it and take it to the ladies' room. He had canvassed and rejected all the natural explanations. For a long time he had toyed with the idea that it contained aids to bedizenment which Miss Corsa reserved for state occasions. Then last week he had come up with the thought of an electric toothbrush, dedicated to special polishing before dental appointments. But would Miss Corsa feel it necessary to rescue her toothbrush?

"Mr. Thatcher?"

It was Captain Rasche, breaking in on this deplorable line of thought. He had finished his tour of the office floors and was prepared to pronounce them uncontaminated by explosives.

"And now for the vaults!"

Everett Gabler wanted one thing clearly understood. "In addition to the examiners and the auditors, there will be two representatives of the bank accompanying your men, Captain!" he said martially. There was no doubt in anyone's mind that he was assigning himself to the party.

"Sure," replied Rasche with heavy pleasantry. "If anything's going to blow up in there, the more the merrier."

Thatcher thought he saw a way to divert his pugnacious subordinate. "Everett," he said gently, "you're worrying about the wrong end of the stick. Has it occurred to you that, if people can introduce things into our vaults, sooner or later they will start thinking about abstracting them?"

Gabler was momentarily speechless.

"Charlie and I will go with Captain Rasche," Thatcher swept on. "I want you to keep an eye on things out here in case of unforeseen trouble."

At the door of the vault they encountered their first problem. The head cashier had not let his tellers leave the main floor until he had collected all cash boxes. Following the usage of years, he wanted to deposit them in the vaults.

"Later, Wilkins," Thatcher said impatiently.

"But what am I supposed to do with them, Mr. Thatcher?" Wilkins wailed. It was against every principle of sound bank procedure to amass the cash boxes in any place except the vaults. "There must be over fifty thousand dollars here!"

"Hold onto them," Thatcher said, sweeping by.

The search of the vaults produced no bombs. It did however produce an occasion for an extempory audit that was hard for certain professionals to resist.

"So this is where you keep your bearer bonds." The examiner was rubbing his hands together with unfeigned interest.

"Not now," said Trinkam and Thatcher in unison.

"If you gentlemen don't mind," Rasche said with terrifying patience, "we still have a lot to do."

"What?" asked Thatcher absently. He was detaching the auditor from a schedule of stock certificates. "We've been everywhere. Mr. Hooper, please! You can come back tomorrow if you insist!"

"We haven't done the safe deposit boxes."

Trinkam was appalled. "You want to open every one of the boxes? Do you know how many we have?" For a moment he was led astray by his own fertile imagination. "Not to mention how the bozoes who rent them will feel about it."

"Look, we have to face facts. If anyone wanted to plant a bomb down here, the easiest way to do it would be to rent a box and put the bomb inside."

Trinkam snorted contemptuously. "So what? We're not talking about an atomic bomb, are we?" He looked at the steel and concrete by which they were surrounded. "It's not going to bring the building down in ruins. Just a little bang-bang and we all go on working."

"No, it wouldn't bring the building down. But it could do a lot of damage to anyone who was standing by it. What if one of your people is just pulling out a box? Want one of them blown up?"

Charlie Trinkam loved his fellow man. "No, no!" he protested. "I don't want anyone hurt. But, my God, all those locked boxes!"

Captain Rasche was unbudging. "There are master keys. There are locksmiths," he said remorselessly. "We've got boys who can drill out a lock."

It was a saddened band that trudged upstairs. Its only accomplishment was to gladden the heart of Mr. Wilkins by waving him back to the vaults. He was gripping his cash boxes with maniacal determination.

Outside Thatcher realized that asking Everett Gabler to look out for trouble was flying in the face of providence.

Everett was standing guard before the double doors. His meager body rigid with indignation, he was confronting a large, smiling man.

"Outrageous!" he was saying.

"Just a little idea," the large man said benignly.

"John," Everett snapped, "this is Mr. Hoffman of the Internal Revenue Service!"

The silence would have done justice to a first-act curtain.

Mr. Hoffman was nothing if not ingratiating. "I understand you'll be opening all your safe deposit boxes. I thought I'd simply tag along with you."

This bloodcurdling suggestion was accompanied by the

deprecatory smile of a man whose wants are so pitiably modest that only a heart of stone could refuse him.

"Not without a court order, you don't!" Thatcher said roundly.

The smile was replaced by pained surprise.

"I wouldn't take notes," he offered hopefully.

"NO!"

Mr. Hoffman shrugged. "We thought it was worth a try," he said philosophically.

"Nicolls!" Thatcher called sternly. "Keep Mr. Hoffman entertained while we are inside."

Kenneth Nicolls, a pleasant young man, was confused but willing. As they left, they heard him asking Hoffman if he liked off-broadway theater.

For once, Thatcher, Charlie Trinkam and Gabler were united. Their deepest instincts as bankers had been threatened. They were all gently seething.

"It's indecent," Gabler said savagely.

"You can't help admiring their gall," Charlie admitted. It was a quality he valued more highly than Gabler did.

"I object to the easy assumption that we are mental defectives." Thatcher was used to more sophisticated ploys from the federal government when it went on the rampage.

"Well," said Charlie, "when you deal with the great American public, it's probably the most useful assumption to make."

Captain Rasche and his locksmiths led the way back downstairs.

Given any large number of safe deposit boxes, the contents are ninety percent predictable and ten percent incomprehensible. The Sloan's were no exception. There were the usual stacks of securities, life insurance policies, wills, and naturalization certificates. In a select-assortment of boxes, there were large bundles of currency, from which everybody tactfully averted their eyes.

"Mafia," Captain Rasche assumed sadly.

"And doctors," Charlie added bracingly.

Then there were obscure little packets which came in for special attention from the bomb squad. None of them contained explosives, detonators, acids or gases under pressure.

"Why do you think anyone keeps an old dog leash here?" Charlie asked the world at large.

Captain Rasche leaped to the defense of the absent animal lover. "A personal memento," he explained. "I remember when Fifi died, I couldn't bring myself to throw out her things. There"—he sighed nostalgically—"there was a poodle!" Then he pointed. "It would be harder to explain what that is doing down here, miles from where it can do any good."

That was a diaphragm.

"Perhaps it, too, is a personal memento." Charlie seemed quite taken with this sentiment. Reverently he closed the box.

Everett Gabler was offended by the entire sordid exchange.

The final review brought to light half a chicken sandwich ("You mean you're going to put it back?"), a passport that was over twenty years out-of-date, packets of letters tied in the traditional pink ribbon ("God, who would have thought anybody was still doing that?"), and report cards for a variety of children who must now be grandparents themselves. The safe deposit boxes received the official seal of approval from Captain Rasche.

"That's that," he announced. "Either it was a hoax, or someone thought they'd get a chance for a break-in, and it didn't work out."

"And in your opinion, Captain, which is the more likely?"

For the first time, Rasche showed signs of fatigue. "We get an average of fifteen false alarms a day. Every nut in town knows this is the way to stir up a lot of excitement. With any other business, I'd say it's nine chances out of ten he's out in the crowd somewhere, having himself a good laugh."

"And with the banking business?"

"Eight chances out of ten," Rasche replied. His opinion of human nature was not high. "You can let your people back into the building now."

Getting them back was easier said than done. In spite of the vigilance of office managers and department supervisors, a surprising number of employees had vanished. A large group of secretaries had last been seen heading for Liberty Street where there was a sale of knitted dresses at Wanamakers. Some of the computer technicians had disappeared into the Doubleday bookstore on Wall Street. Far too many trust officers had directed their steps to the nearest bar.

"Just as I feared," said Thatcher when this was reported to him. "Only the technicians read."

"But, Mr. Thatcher," exclaimed the personnel manager, who did not understand what he was talking about, "how am I going to explain all this on the day sheets? I'm sure the Board will want to know."

Thatcher had already foreseen the inevitable meeting of the Board of Directors. But there was another question-and-answer session scheduled first.

Captain Rasche wanted to have a little talk.

20

VINEGAR TO THE TEETH

Thatcher led Captain Rasche indoors. The Sloan Guaranty Trust now resembled nothing so much as an overturned hive. Upstairs in the Trust Department, conversational knots were strung along the whole corridor. The passage of John Putnam Thatcher, with a party of policemen, went virtually unnoticed in the buzz of emotions compared, adventures described and philosophy expounded.

Rasche waxed expert.

"Your first threat, I see," he remarked as they walked on. Innes from International could be heard topping everybody with reminiscences of Guatemala where bombings are really bombings.

Thatcher admitted that, until now, the Sloan had been spared the attention of terrorists.

"It shows." Rasche nodded sagely. "Your people still get excited. After they've been through it once or twice, they'll get pretty blasé. Then too, if we have to clear the building when it's raining hard—well, you'll hear a lot of talk about lynching."

Thatcher resolutely banished the prospect of trying to run the bank as the staff trooped in and out to Exchange Place. Fortunately Miss Corsa, in the outer office, was a study in normalcy. Presumably her little tin box was safe in its drawer. To the naked eye, all looked well.

Except, of course, for the note that Captain Rasche examined quickly, then handed on to his aide.

"St. Bernadette's," he read aloud. "Of course, they've been getting themselves some real publicity. It's possible that somebody just took advantage of it and used their name. That's the way I'd normally figure it. Except . . ."

He broke off, but Thatcher had no difficulty finishing the sentence.

Except for murder.

Rasche returned his attention. Experience, he told Thatcher, suggested that the note itself would offer scant help. There would be no fingerprints—or too many.

"What we'll try to do," he began, "is trace how it got to you."

"Perhaps we can help." Thatcher rang for Miss Corsa.

She was ahead of them.

"I thought about that," she reported, suggesting somehow that Thatcher and Rasche had been wasting time. "The note didn't come through the outside mail. There was no stamp. And it was addressed to you by name, Mr. Thatcher—with no title or address. Only sixth floor. So I asked Sheldon. And he asked Manuel . . ."

The note had been deposited in the Sloan's night drop sometime after the close of business yesterday. Early this morning, it had been collected, routed to the mail room, and delivered to Miss Corsa's desk by the time she arrived.

"Fine," said Rasche. "We'll check with the night men. Maybe one of them noticed something last night."

"I doubt it," Thatcher commented. Hundreds of men and firms on Wall Street made use of the Sloan's night deposit. Hence there was a fairly broad surveillance during the hours when Wall Street was silent, deserted and dangerous for anybody carrying large sums of cash. But during the rush

hour, when thousands of men and women scurried past the
Sloan to catch the subway, no one could ever identify a
single figure slipping an envelope into a slot.

"And we'll check out the whole St. Bernadette's crowd,"
Rasche was going on. "I've already been in touch with
Homicide. But one thing—this sixth-floor business. How many
people know your office is on the sixth floor?"

Thatcher was trying to recall when he became conscious
that Miss Corsa was still in the doorway. Since Miss Corsa
was never uncertain, this could only mean she had something to offer.

"Yes, Miss Corsa?" he broke off to ask.

"The note did say *down with all enemies of St. Bernadette's,*" she reminded them. "Shouldn't they be warned?"

"Now who would the enemies of St. Bernadette's be, I
wonder?" Captain Rasche asked the world.

"Unger Realty," Miss Corsa informed at once. "And the
Chancery as well."

This effectively put an end to Rasche's relaxation. Hur-
riedly, he got to his feet, informed Thatcher that further inquiries would be pursued, and departed.

"But if that note was sent by anybody connected with St.
Bernadette's," Thatcher mused aloud, "what did he hope to
gain by creating a bomb scare here at the Sloan?"

Miss Corsa had a literal mind. "It stopped all work for a
long time," she observed.

"I trust, Miss Corsa, that you are not being sarcastic at
my expense," said Thatcher. "As long as you're here, let's
get started. I'll have to see the department heads . . ."

Even as he made arrangements for an immediate tally of
the damage, Thatcher pondered Miss Corsa's words. How
could interrupting the Sloan's work help anybody at St.
Bernadette's? Anybody at all.

But the next two hours gave him little opportunity to explore this line of thought. Almost immediately, the department heads filed in, big with woe and lamentation. It was
surprising what havoc had been wrought. For the first time
in recorded history, the Sloan had unwittingly contravened
several stringent requirements of local and national banking
law. Specific instructions from clients had gone undischarged.

The bond market had fallen apart. Deadlines had lost all meaning. Both Mellish, from Reserve Accounting, and Bannerman, from Federal Funds, were beyond lucid speech.

Everett Gabler was not. ". . . and furthermore, three trust officers have completely disappeared. Among them, I regret to say, is Trinkam."

"Look on it," Thatcher advised idly, "as a long lunch hour. Now, about this daily clearing report . . ."

Getting the Sloan back on even keel was not easy. Thatcher was giving brutally direct orders about collateral when Miss Corsa rang through.

"No, Miss Corsa, you'd better hold my calls," he said impatiently. He had a very fair notion how this morning's adventure would strike too many of his friends and acquaintances.

Miss Corsa was severe. "I have already told Mr. Robichaux, Mr. Waymark and Mrs. Withers that you will return their calls later this afternoon."

"Fine, fine," said Thatcher, penciling a list that Bannerman proffered with a shaking hand.

"This," continued Miss Corsa inexorably, "is Mr. Unger. I think you will wish to speak to him. He is calling from a pay phone in a drugstore . . ."

Before Thatcher could digest her last words, an hysterical voice broke over him.

"A bomb!" said Unger. "Thank God Dad isn't here!"

"Is it a real bomb—or simply the threat of a bomb?" Thatcher intervened to save time. Everybody in his office, he noticed, looked up. Even Bannerman became less morose. There was no doubt about it. Misery loves company.

"They're searching now," Unger mumbled distractedly. "They've cleared everybody out of the whole building. You can't imagine the mess—"

"Oh, yes I can," said Thatcher grimly. "We had our own bomb threat this morning."

Unger was not interested in what happened at the Sloan. Thatcher broke in on a disjointed plaint.

"Did you get a warning note?"

Unger Realty had not received a note. A disguised voice had reached the switchboard just after lunch. Before succumbing to shock, Myrtle reported two sentences: *You've got a bomb in your office. You're not going to destroy St. Bernadette's.*

"Hmm," said Thatcher.

"My God! What kind of people throw bombs—just because of some lousy real estate?" Unger's voice trembled. "What kind . . ."

This was no time to explain that St. Bernadette's was more than a piece of real estate. Furthermore, if Thatcher had any appetite for temperamental outbursts, he could satisfy it in his own office.

"Well, I wish you luck," he said unsympathetically. "Let me know if you have an explosion."

He hung up without further ado.

Everett left his truants for the moment. "A bomb threat at Unger Realty? Surely that proves this is all tied to St. Bernadette's, don't you agree?"

"I should think so," said Thatcher. It was a shame. Everett would obviously prefer anarchists. "Have we got an interim report for the Federal Reserve?"

Forty minutes later, Miss Corsa reappeared and said, "It was another hoax at Unger Realty. They didn't find a bomb."

Thatcher looked up from the draft he and Bannerman were hammering out.

"Good," he said absently. "Keep me abreast of what happens to the Chancery too, won't you, Miss Corsa?"

She did not conceal her deep disapproval of nonchalance on such a subject.

"Mr. Gaven from Communications wants to speak to you," she said, ignoring his last observation. "He was in an anti-demolition unit during the war. He wants to know if he can organize a Sloan Bomb Squad."

"Tell him," said Thatcher with careful control, "to send me a memo."

The next thing would be a Sloan Vigilante Committee, challenging the Glee Club for members. Why not? Everybody else was going crazy. Why expect the Great Sloan Family to be immune?

". . . what was that, Everett?"

There followed a complex proposition for shifting any

liability the Sloan might have incurred to other shoulders—any shoulders. Everett was barely finished before Miss Corsa was back.

"Now what?" Thatcher demanded before it dawned on him that Miss Corsa was looking shaken. It had been, after all, a long, hard day.

"It just came over the ticker," she announced.

Thatcher glanced down at his watch. The market had closed hours ago without further collapse. Could war have been declared?

"They're evacuating the Chancery," Miss Corsa said hollowly. "Somebody's threatened to bomb the Cardinal!"

It was late in the evening before Thatcher felt free to call a halt. All that man could do had now been done. With luck, the Sloan should be able to face the morrow as if today had never been.

"All bark and no bite," Charlie Trinkam commented. He had drifted back to work with his customary insouciance. Now he was sitting on the corner of Thatcher's desk, taking part in a casual postmortem.

Miss Corsa cast him a look of burning reproach which he interpreted correctly.

"Come on, Rose," he cajoled. "It was only another hoax at the Chancery, wasn't it? Nobody blew anybody up."

Since this was true, Miss Corsa fell back on dignity. Was that, she asked Mr. Thatcher, all?

"Yes," said Thatcher. There was no use thanking Miss Corsa for her heroic performance. The way to do so was by a gift. Not even Miss Corsa could brush aside some splendid object from Bergdorf's.

"It's a neat twist," Charlie observed.

Walter Bowman, smothering a yawn, asked for an explanation.

Charlie expanded. "Here we are, going crazy with bomb threats all day long. The Sloan closes down. Unger has gone crackers, from what I hear. And when they had to evacuate the Chancery—well, they just about sealed off midtown. They got so many cops and firemen over there that all traffic between Forty-second Street and Central Park ground to a stop. They're just breaking up the jam now."

It had, everybody agreed, been a memorable day.

"And it's all because of some dummy worked up about St. Bernadette's, right?" Charlie went on.

Thatcher replied that was a reasonable presumption.

"Well," Charlie resumed, "you can bet your bottom dollar there's no excitement at St. Bernadette's. You know Flensburg types. The original good citizens. They're sitting around watching TV. They're going to bed early. If there's any excitement at all up there, it's a whist party at the rectory."

Charlie for one preferred a bomb threat to a whist party any day.

He was, however, inaccurate. It was not whist. It was beano.

". . . Number . . . twenty . . . two," called out the man on the platform.

Groans, delighted cries, intent silence. At long banks of tables, men and women studied their cards, then looked up to watch number twenty-two being chalked on the blackboard behind the revolving wheel.

"Everybody ready? The next . . . number . . . is . . . number . . . eight . . . eight . . ."

Prominently displayed beside the caller were the prizes wrested by the sodality from Flensburg merchants: a toaster, two canned hams, a painted china lamp and a clock radio. But the half-hundred St. Bernadette's parishioners who regularly gathered for the weekly game were drawn as much by the desire for simple sociability as by the hope of something for nothing.

From the door, Father Doyle looked on with approval. He did not share Charlie Trinkam's view of the world. Flensburg quiet, Flensburg seeking its excitement in a friendly game of beano—this was the Flensburg Father Doyle knew and loved. Just as he loved the Flensburg already home in bed, at ten o'clock in the evening.

". . . number twenty-six . . . twenty-six . . ."

"BEANO!"

Mrs. Lento jumped up. "Beano! After six straight weeks!"

Around her rose a hum of cheerful disappointment, of congratulations.

A fine scene, Father Doyle rejoiced. Happy. Peaceful. The way it should be.

While Mrs. Lento went up to collect her clock radio, Father Doyle decided to duck outdoors for a breath of air. With a rare sense of well-being, he gazed up and down Jackson Boulevard. Quiet and peaceful here too. Whatever was happening elsewhere, Flensburg was not a battleground.

"And thanks for mercies rendered," said Father Doyle to himself. He was turning to go back indoors when he heard it.

There was one sharp report. Then silence.

Bewildered, he shook his head. Jackson Boulevard was still quiet. His old ears, he decided, must be playing tricks.

Suddenly he went rigid. From inside the parish hall, there came the drumming of many feet.

"Mary, Mother of God!" he croaked.

There was a breathless voice behind him. "Father, did you hear something?"

Father Doyle could only stare at the man. Somebody ran out into the parking lot. Frantically he pointed.

A dull red glare pulsated in the sky.

"Fire!" somebody shouted.

There was a concerted rush past Father Doyle.

"Fire! The school's on fire!"

"Where's the fire alarm?"

And finally in the fearful excitement, there was another voice.

"It's a bomb!" screamed a woman. "They've bombed St. Bernadette's."

21

COALS OF FIRE

Within moments the schoolyard and parking lot were thronged.

The beano players, naturally, were first on the scene, leaving behind them overturned chairs, scattered score cards, the chewed stumps of pencils and the lamp which was to have been the next prize. Even the wheel used for drawing numbers was knocked from its stand in the hasty exodus.

But they were soon joined by others who had heard the blast or seen the brilliant flash. Most shops across Jackson Boulevard were closed for the night. Phil Kavanaugh, however, had been spending a rare evening at work. He was culling unsold paperbacks to be returned to the distributor. (It was his boast that every single volume on display had been approved by Sister Veronica. Sister Veronica was too wise to ask what was under the counter.) When the explosion came, Kavanaugh stiffened. For several seconds he remained bent over a pile of books, with only his head raised. His eyes glittered. Then he hurried to the sidewalk and broke into an awkward, angular trot.

The Parents League headquarters had also been occupied. Weeks ago a young couple had volunteered to check returned questionnaires. Even before the police had relinquished the store front, the Connors had picked up Mary Foster's master list, gathered the mail from the post office and set to work. Riots and tenants' crusades had come and gone. Unnoticed, the Connors continued their self-appointed task. Just as their work became irrelevant, they finished it. (Question: Why do you wish to send your child to St. Bernadette's? Check one of the four boxes below. Question: How much would you be willing to pay to continue sending your child

COALS OF FIRE 163

to St. Bernadette's? The figures below represent weekly payment per child.) They had triumphantly filed their summary and were locking the front door when Joan Connor pointed and seized her husband's arm. With great presence of mind Ed Connor rushed inside and called the fire department.

The nuns in the convent beyond the playground were leaving their chapel after the last service of the day. They were in the habit of chatting for a few minutes before retiring. ("Why are suppers so much worse when Sister Columba plans them? I know it's good for Sister Columba to mortify herself by performing an uncongenial duty. But what about the rest of us? Couldn't Reverend Mother assign Sister Columba a different duty? Like polishing the silver?") They saw, they gasped, they rushed forward.

All these people were in the schoolyard by the time the windows of the small annex were reflecting a ruddy glow. Their numbers were soon swelled by firemen, local residents, and several steadies from the Galway Tavern. Newcomers soon heard about the bang and the flash. Everybody noticed that the fire fighters were quickly reinforced by technicians— from the fire marshal's office and the police bomb squad. Teenagers in the crowd turned up their transistor radios when the inevitable spot announcement came:

"We interrupt this program. A bomb has just exploded at St. Bernadette's Catholic School in Flensburg. Earlier today bomb threats were received at St. Patrick's Chancery, the Sloan Guaranty Trust and Unger Realty . . ."

An hour later St. Bernadette's was no longer recognizable. Trampling feet and rivers of water had churned the yard into a sea of mud. Everywhere, heavy hoses being recoiled were a hazard. Broken glass and crumbling ash surrounded the blackened shell of the annex. Smoke, still hanging like a pall over the building, reeked of charred wood.

The fire fighting was over. The main block of the school had been saved. Even the ruined annex was still structurally sound. But hip-booted men continued searching through the debris. Every now and then an object was retrieved and carried to the bomb squad. Most of Flensburg was now milling around the disaster area and overheard the conclusions being drawn.

"It's not hard to see how this was set up. The annex is a large room with a kitchenette. The mothers take turns supervising lunch hour. Somebody used a Molotov cocktail with this primitive fuse. But the pilot on the gas stove was extinguished with the taps left open. That's where the explosion came from. Luckily the fuse was only good for about five minutes. Otherwise there would have been a big enough blast to bring the annex down."

The implications of this speech were horrifying enough to reach the very edges of the crowd in minutes.

"Did you hear what he said? That *was* a bomb in the school!"

"What if the kids had been there? They could all have been killed!"

"They made a mistake with the fuse. They were trying to bring down the whole school!"

"My God, what kind of a monster do we have in Flensburg?"

Several people were swift to draw the same conclusion as the radio announcer.

"You heard about the bomb scares they had today over at St. Pat's and that bank? Well, this is the same thing—"

Someone was outraged at the comparison.

"What do you mean, it's the same thing? There weren't any bombs in those other places!"

A mother went further. "And there weren't any kids! My God, this must be a maniac."

Then, off to one side, there were shouts of a different description.

"Hey! Make room up there! Father Doyle's coming." The crowd split, creating an aisle which led to the bomb squad. At the end of it Father Doyle appeared, supported by Mary Foster and the Ianellos. He tottered as he walked, confused and bewildered. But he spoke with the stubborn insistence of a man who will not believe what he hears.

"No, no. There must be some mistake. What are you about, letting everybody spread these lies?"

Sal Ianello was holding one of his arms. "Now, Father," he said soothingly, "I know it's terrible, but you mustn't—".

Father Doyle jerked his arm away. "Don't be a fool!" he

snapped. "You're like children, all of you. Wanting to drama-
tize things! There's been a fire, that's all. Someone was
careless."

Quietly Ianello replaced his hand. Father Doyle did not
seem to notice. He was muttering to himself now. "A fire,
that's what it must be."

Over his head, Mary Foster and the Ianellos exchanged
anguished glances. Sal bobbed his head toward Mary, indi-
cating that she should take over. The priest would be more
comfortable talking to a woman.

Mary went to work immediately. "The fire is out now,
Father. The engines came right away and it didn't take them
more than twenty minutes to handle the worst of it." She
tried hard to banish any suggestion of the cheerful nurse as
she urged the party forward. "These are the men who were
in charge. We owe them a lot."

The fire marshal and the head of the bomb squad came
forward to meet them.

"And who would you be?" Father Doyle demanded.

They identified themselves.

"Now we'll have the truth of it," the priest grunted with
satisfaction. "Tell them this business about a bomb is nonsense."

The two men were sympathetic but firm. Patiently they
produced evidence, outlined their reasoning, and explained
about fuses and gas concentrations.

"I'm afraid there isn't any doubt, Father," the marshal
said with kind finality. "Anybody could figure out how to do
it. The whole thing could have been rigged up in a couple
of minutes."

At first Father Doyle struggled, his eyes flickering away
from the length of fuse, his head averted from the gaping
window frames of the annex. But the last remorseless words
seemed to overtax his strength. He sagged against his companions.

"Who is there in my parish," he asked himself, "who could
do such a thing?"

"Father Doyle!" Mary Foster cried. "This is too much for
you! You should be resting."

The priest drew on his last reserves of will power. He

tried to draw himself erect. "I must know how this happened. I must know everything about it. Then maybe I will understand why."

Sal Ianello was gentle. "Yes, of course, Father. But these men are still working. I'll find out everything and tell you tomorrow morning." He started to turn the old man around. "But now, there are Mrs. Dewey and Father James waiting to take you home. You must rest tonight."

The rectory housekeeper had been hovering on the outskirts of the group for some time. She and Father James came forward together.

"I'm an old man," Father Doyle said pathetically. "I'm too old to understand all this."

Mrs. Dewey slipped an arm around him and he allowed himself to be led back to the rectory. Father James brought up the rear.

The crowd watched them go in silence. Then there was a collective sigh. Before Father Doyle came they had been excited and aghast. Now the first rumblings of collective anger began.

"Are we going to take this? What if this guy decides to have another crack?"

"We were lucky this time. But we have to protect the kids. We may not be so lucky next time."

As the first call for action was raised, two newcomers burst onto the scene. They came loping down Jackson Boulevard together, but at the entrance to the schoolyard they split. Bob Horvath headed straight for his fellow parishioners. Willard Ericson made a beeline for the officials.

"My God, is it true?" Horvath demanded. "I didn't know a thing about it. But Ericson caught the news flash, and he came straight out. He picked me up on the way."

Eager voices were quick to assure him it was all true, to repeat what the marshal had said, to describe how Father Doyle was a broken man.

"It was awful," said Pat Ianello, still pale. "Poor Father Doyle! He aged twenty years right in front of us."

"That's tough," Horvath agreed readily. "I hope he'll be all right."

Everybody said that Father Doyle was no longer a young man. It would take time for him to recover from the shock.

"I told him I'd find out everything I could," Sal said, "and tell him all about it tomorrow morning."

"Yeah, sure." Bob Horvath was frowning. "Of course, he's got a right to know. But look, Sal, we can't expect too much from Father Doyle. It wouldn't be right to load him with our problems."

Sal stared. "What do you mean? He's the priest, isn't he?"

"Sure he is. But he doesn't really understand what's going on. And he doesn't know much about courts and television and that sort of thing. What I mean to say is that we don't have to wait until tomorrow morning. We've got Mr. Ericson here right now."

This news was a tonic to the crowd.

"Let's see what Mr. Ericson has got to say," someone shouted from the rear.

"Go on, Bob," a woman urged. "Get him over here."

But Willard Ericson had already finished with the fire marshal. He was bustling forward. From every corner of the schoolyard, parents hurried to swell the crowd around him. They were tense with anticipation.

Precise as ever, Ericson looked over his glasses at his audience.

"The marshal has assured me that the explosion was deliberately caused by a bomb. It was a very simple contrivance apparently, available to anyone."

They knew this already. But they remained hopeful. Experience had proved that Willard Ericson was a slow starter. He liked to review the obvious.

"So we run no danger of being suspected of irresponsible accusations. Now is the time to strive for maximum publicity. We have nothing to lose and everything to gain. The sympathetic response will be enormous. No television viewer will regard the parents of St. Bernadette's as anything but victims."

Ericson had lost contact with his clients. He was far too able a lawyer not to sense this. Unfortunately he could not imagine why. He paused, trying to assess the feelings around him. There was nothing definite. Only that slight, silent with-drawal.

Mary Foster was the one who spoke up. "But Mr. Eric-son," she said tautly, "there are no television cameras here."

Could this be what was bothering them? Ericson hast-ened to reassure her.

"We'll get them here. By tomorrow morning we could probably arrange a special half-hour on the bombing. There won't be any difficulty."

Sal Ianello was choking with rage. "Are you crazy or something? Telling us we've got nothing to lose? I've got a little girl going to St. Bernadette's."

Too late, Ericson tried to consider this aspect of the situa-tion. "But, Mr. Ianello," he protested, "your little girl isn't going to be affected by a publicity campaign about the bombings. I don't—"

"I don't want a publicity carnival about these bombings," Sal raged. "I don't want to attract every nut in the city. I want to stop the bombings!"

There was no doubt about the sentiment of the crowd. Cries of encouragement rose on all sides. Bob Horvath was looking at Ericson in stunned disappointment. Mary Foster had moved a few paces away from him.

"That's telling them, Sal!"

"You can count on me, Sal!"

"We don't need a lot of outsiders making hay from this!"

But there were some who wanted more details. How, they asked, was Sal going to go about things? What could they do?

"I'll tell you if you'll all shut up!"

Unconsciously, the circle was reforming. At its center was Sal Ianello. Pat and Mary Foster stood near him. Only Bob Horvath was still watching Willard Ericson.

"The first thing we've got to do is start guarding the school. This wouldn't have happened tonight if we'd had some sort of a watch."

Here was a limited objective within their powers. Parents worried about their children were being offered the oppor-tunity to do something effective. Enthusiastically they offered their services.

"No, hear me out!" Sal held up a restraining hand. "We've

got to organize this. There are over a hundred fathers with children in the school. We'll set up shifts. Everybody will take a turn."

"Mothers too!" a woman called.

Grimly Sal continued to cleave his way through distractions. "All right, mothers too. But the main point is that the school should be guarded every minute, day and night. No one gets into St. Bernadette's with bottles or packages of any kind. We'll set up a checking station if we have to."

"I just hope the bastard tries again," a father said threateningly. "If I'm on duty, he won't be in shape to play those tricks ever again."

Other fathers echoed him.

"And no outsiders," someone suggested. "Even if they're not carrying anything. No one but parents and teachers get anywhere near the school. That'll do the trick."

Bob Horvath had shifted allegiance. Abandoning Willard Ericson, he called out, "Put me down, Sal. Any time of the night. You've got this thing licked."

"Oh, no, I haven't!"

The excited chirpings came to a halt. What was Sal saying?

"Listen to me! Having guards at the school is only temporary. Sure, we can do it for a week, maybe a month. But we can't do it forever."

"We can try!" they promised loyally.

"Sure, we'll try," Sal rejoined. "But we don't want to turn St. Bernadette's into some kind of jail. We want a normal school, like we used to have. And I'll tell you one thing. All this trouble started because the Cardinal wants to sell the school. Well, it was one thing when it was a question of money. I didn't agree with the Cathedral, but I could see how they were thinking in terms of dollars and cents. But things are different now. They're playing with the lives and safety of our children. We've got to make them see that."

The chorus of approval was deafening.

"The Cardinal will have to back down now. There isn't any other way of looking at things any more. Not when people are throwing bombs. If they need money, let them sell some other school."

Cheers!

The voice was a hoarse croak by now. "So we're going to want two lists. While some of us are guarding the school, the rest of us are going to have to go in to St. Patrick's. We'll make them see things our way if we have to picket Mass on Sunday! I want as many of you as can come. And I want everybody—men, women, grandparents, teenagers. I want Monsignor Miles to see that all of St. Bernadette's is standing together. And we expect the Church to stand with us!"

Sal Ianello was a man who had found his hour.

22

THERE IS NO REST

Many Flensburg fathers did not go to work the following morning. This was only to be expected. But the aftermath of the bombing disrupted other schedules as well. John Thatcher did not reach his office until after eleven o'clock. Charlie Trinkam, encountering him at the elevator, hovered on the brink of pleasantry. One quick look was enough to recommend prudence.

"Good morning, John," Trinkam said sedately.

"Good morning, Charlie."

Charlie escaped unscathed to pass the word: all signs pointed to a bad day.

Miss Corsa was not so fortunate.

"Good morning, Mr. Thatcher," she said.

It was enough.

"I realize that I have missed an appointment," Thatcher declaimed. "Let me assure you that I did not oversleep. On the contrary."

Miss Corsa withheld comment.

"Since early this morning—very early this morning—I

have been occupied with St. Bernadette's," said Thatcher, shrugging off his coat. "First it was a phone call from Ericson. This was followed by calls from the police. Then Unger. Finally the papers. I have already refused to make any public statement on behalf of the Sloan four times. Furthermore, I have arranged for doubling—if not trebling—our security guard for the duration."

Miss Corsa knew her duty. "*The New York Times* would like to interview—"

"Miss Corsa!" said Thatcher wrathfully. "I have had enough of St. Bernadette's, enough of Catholic parochial schools, enough of the entire Archdiocese of New York! I am certainly giving no interviews on the subject. Will you please remember that? I do not want to be reminded of St. Bernadette's in any way, shape or form—for what little remains of the morning! Or, if you can manage it, for the rest of the year!"

"Certainly, Mr. Thatcher," said the perfect secretary. "Are you ready to see Mr. Bowman now?"

"Send him in," Thatcher ordered.

By ill chance, Walter had not been alerted by Trinkam. He breezed past Miss Corsa.

"Morning, John! Say, that's a surprise, isn't it—that bombing out in Flensburg? After yesterday, I was willing to bet that some joker was running around just trying to scare everybody. But not trying hard enough to use real bombs. Then—*powee!* And that's another thing. We had three big bomb warnings. But when the one bomb comes—it's out of the blue. No warning at all, according to the radio this morning. Do you suppose . . . ?"

Belatedly, the prevailing chill penetrated. Walter trailed off.

"I think," said Thatcher bleakly, "that we'll leave bombs and bombers to the authorities. Now, about that forecast you were going to show me."

Walter, nobody's fool, darted immediately into the work at hand. "Here you are. They've just revised the first quarter estimates. I've come up with a higher figure for plant and equipment expenditures."

For twenty praiseworthy minutes, Thatcher took Bowman back and forth over a compendium of important economic statistics. This arid exercise provided the taskmaster with a measure of grim satisfaction. It also revived Walter.

"Okay," he said, rising to leave. "I'll circulate this to Trust and Investment. Of course, they're all so gloomy right now, it would take manna from heaven to cheer them up. One thing I'm not going to tell them. I've just realized that this is the longest bear market we've had since 1929. Makes you stop and think, doesn't it?"

"What does it make you think?" Thatcher asked. This was not sarcasm. No matter what his mood, he was never inclined to undervalue Bowman.

Walter grew reflective. "We-ell," he said. "For one thing, most people don't notice much. Not unless there's a sign telling them what they should look for. Then too, it makes me think that Wall Street has specialists in counting trees. But they're great at missing forests! And finally"—he grinned —"I think about the ten or twelve guys who cottoned on to the bear market early—the ones who made a mint selling short."

He checked to see if Thatcher was interested. "You know, we've had the big black headlines about the losers. When McConnell"—the giant brokerage house—"went bankrupt. When we had those rumors about Frederick I. Dumont. When Whetstone Fund lost $42 million—and I still don't understand how they managed to do that. I guess that's Boston for you! But what I really would like to find out is who are the boys who made the money."

Thatcher nodded. Like Bowman, he knew that even during the worst stock market debacles some people make money. They do not make headlines.

Walter summed up. "During the Flood, somebody probably was making a fast buck. The guy who subcontracted that ark made the profits. He let Noah keep the publicity. Well, thanks, John."

He left Thatcher feeling insensibly less antagonistic toward the whole world.

"Miss Corsa," he told the intercom, "we can get to that file of correspondence you were complaining about the other day."

For certain letters, there is a time. It had come. In moments, Thatcher was giving his preliminary cough:

> DEAR BEN: We have read with interest your suggestion that you transfer outright your common stock of MidWestern Railroad to the employees. We note the line is incurring heavy deficits. While we agree that such a transfer holds tax advantages, there are other concerns . . .

He proceeded briskly, flattening several disingenuous schemes in rapid succession.

By mid-afternoon, Thatcher had made substantial inroads on the backlog despite his late start. This should have been balm to his soul. For several unbroken hours, thanks to Miss Corsa's intercepts, he had been allowed to forget Flensburg. But it was easier to lay down the law to others than to discipline his own reprehensible curiosity.

True, one portion of Thatcher was sated with the endless ramifications flowing from Unger's ill-omened plan to purchase St. Bernadette's and replace it with an apartment building. That modest edifice had already consumed more Sloan time and attention than an entire New Town outside Washington, D.C.—which the bank was also financing.

But there was another side to Thatcher. Despite his ferocity on the subject, he found events in Flensburg anomalous enough to spark the same inquisitive demon stirred by Miss Corsa's little tin box.

Alone in his office, with a distant typewriter providing background music, he bridged his fingers, swiveled around, and gazed unseeingly out the window. Half-hearted mid-March snowflakes straggled down through a steel-gray gloom.

If he had to put a word to these St. Bernadette's dramatics, it would not be one of the inflammatory adjectives empurpling local press and television. It would be *improbable*. No doubt, parent protests were foreseeable whenever the sale of a parochial school was proposed.

But was murder?

Thatcher frowned. Furthermore, Omara's murder had been the first, not the culminating, touch of the grotesque. Perhaps, in a world of instant social response, Catholic modernists rioting on the steps of the church were just as predictable.

But what explained the overnight transformation of enraged parents into disgruntled tenants? It was, after all, a long step from SAVE ST. BERNADETTE'S to TAR AND FEATHER SIRIUS MEEKS!

And last, but not least, there were three bomb threats, and the enormous confusion they had created from Exchange Place to Madison Avenue.

Plus one actual bomb, which had damaged the very school whose preservation had triggered this entire fracas.

"I wonder how the Flensburg parents are responding to this?" Thatcher wondered to himself.

Respond they would, he knew. The Flensburg parents were a volatile crew. First it had been St. Bernadette's. Then absentee landlords. Now with a threat to their children? Two to one—it would be back to St. Bernadette's.

Thatcher tried to decide whether this represented a pattern or simply a demented game of Ping-Pong played by obscure rules. Just then the outside world intruded. Mr. Withers, Miss Corsa announced, was on the line. This time from Bulawayo.

Modern communications had much to answer for, Thatcher discovered. News of the bomb threat to the Sloan had reached the Sloan's wandering president even on the Dark Continent.

"No, no," Thatcher reassured his chief. "There is absolutely no need for you to cut short this trip, Brad."

"In an emergency," said the overseas voice ringingly, "I want to be at my post."

After considering several possible replies to this, Thatcher turned the conversation as soon as he could. Bradford Withers' interest in banking was always fitful. Just now it paled by comparison.

"A safari?" Thatcher repeated politely. "Yes, indeed. It does sound more . . . more challenging than touring Mongolia."

Bradford Withers was not uniformly unreconstructed. "A photographic safari, John, I need scarcely explain. There will be no senseless slaughter."

"Excellent!" said Thatcher, recalling Withers' various High-land shooting jaunts and Norwegian fishing forays. He listened to the coming attractions. There would be White Hunters. There would be Native Bearers. There would be camps pitched in Jungle Clearings. There would be Big Game.

It needed only Rider Haggard.

"But I didn't call to talk about myself," Brad lied. "I really wanted to be sure that this violence does not demand my presence."

"No, everything's under control," Thatcher said heartily. "Don't worry, Brad. And . . . er . . . good shooting."

He hung up. Tastes vary, but it still was strange that any-body should spend thousands of dollars on stage props. Brad Withers, like many another tourist before him, was going to end up pointing a camera at something. That it would be the most expensive camera Germany had ever produced did not, in Thatcher's view, alter facts. Yet for Withers, the props made the difference. Fake hunting for fake hunters.

Fake danger and fake violence.

Suddenly Thatcher again swiveled around to inspect the oppressive weather. Walter Bowman had been talking about natural camouflage. Bradford Withers was contriving his own.

Did that fit St. Bernadette's? Murder, riots, bombing?

What if they, too, were contrived effects? What if the im-portant thing was that pattern he had discerned earlier: St. Bernadette's—landlords—St. Bernadette's?

A banker, thought Thatcher, might have a good explana-tion for such a pattern—and a better one than the police had.

Certainly a banker could think of a very quick way to test his hypothesis.

He stabbed the buzzer.

"Miss Corsa," he said, "I want you to drop whatever you're doing. I have a few calls for you to make."

Miss Corsa found him deep in thought.

"Now, let's see," he said, casting his mind back. "First of all, the Real Estate Board. Then I'd like you to contact this man Kavanaugh. He owns a candy store out in Flensburg. Then . . . just possibly . . . you might call Mrs. Omara. That's Mrs. Francis Omara."

When he fleshed out his instructions, Miss Corsa gave him a long appraising look.

"And what are you going to do, Mr. Thatcher?"

There were several possibilities. "I can think of two people I might talk to. I'll start with the one nearest to hand."

She looked up.

"Monsignor Miles," he said. "Will you see if he has any free time this afternoon?"

One of his questions was answered before Thatcher got out of the taxi at the corner of Madison and Fiftieth. The bomb at St. Bernadette's had galvanized Flensburg.

"Geeze!" exclaimed the cabbie. "They just got rid of the grave diggers picketing the Cardinal's residence. Now they got this!"

Three hundred mothers and fathers parading solemnly around St. Patrick's Cathedral and the Chancery. Marching four abreast, they paced out a giant figure eight. Since this involved crossing and recrossing Madison Avenue, traffic was as effectively snarled as it had been by the firetrucks and patrol cars of yesterday.

Even as Thatcher and the cabbie looked on, police reinforcements sped up. Flensburg parents could not be bothered with permits or traffic control. Homemade placards proclaimed a new iron in the community soul:

SUFFER THE LITTLE CHILDREN
IS MONEY MORE PRECIOUS THAN BLOOD?
NO HUMAN SACRIFICES!

New York had seen larger, more impassioned public demonstrations. Yet the men and women of Flensburg were impressive beyond their numbers. Even casual bystanders could see that this was no haphazard outpouring. Every marcher was deeply serious. Four nuns, carrying a large banner, were tight-lipped, grave and determined.

Behind them, row after row of parents filed, just as somber. There were no bizarrely clad adolescents. There were few beards. Most of the women were dressed conservatively enough to be coming from Mass. Many of the men wore

work clothes. And there were uniforms as well: a subway con-
ductor, several mechanics, a milkman. The whole parade was
demonstrably adult.

Many of the sternly set faces that passed before the taxi
were vaguely familiar to Thatcher. Behind the nuns, for example, marched the young A&P manager, Sal Ianello. Hatless,
he was frowning ahead. His lower lip jutted out. At his side,
his wife Pat was solemn.

As Ianello disappeared across the street, Thatcher was reminded of something. For a moment, he could not put his
finger on it. Then it came.

Sal Ianello, thin, slight, and essentially modest, had become Napoleonic.

Were others transformed, too? Thatcher craned his neck.

Just coming into view were the Horvaths. Bob Horvath
lumbered along, his shoulders hunched in his jacket. Mrs.
Horvath was wearing a modish fur hat and high heels.
Neither of them seemed much changed. Horvath looked
stolid, almost stupid. Occasionally, Ruthie said something
to him. From where he stood, Thatcher could not see if her
husband replied.

"Hey!" said the cabbie, fishing for change. "They even
got the priest!"

Startled, Thatcher looked up. He could not believe that
Father Doyle would picket St. Patrick's.

It was Father James. He strode along, out of step, almost
treading on the heels of the people ahead of him. That conscious defiance also reminded Thatcher of something. Not
Napoleon. Possibly St. Stephen.

The cabbie had some big-city philosophy to impart.

"You got to hand it to them Catholics. The way they stick
together."

This was not the way Thatcher interpreted a united show
of opposition to Joseph, Cardinal Devlin and the archdiocesan hierarchy. But he knew what the driver meant.

The procession did symbolize a profound common concern. There, marching with several other women, for instance, was Mary Foster. She was as resolute as everybody
else. Flensburg was no longer divided.

"Not that I blame them," said the cabbie, pocketing a substantial tip. "That's a helluva thing. Throwing bombs at little kids."

Thatcher let him go without observing that a small bomb late at night was not a major peril to schoolchildren. The symbol and the precedent were too powerful.

Monsignor Miles spelled it out. "They are outraged and angry. Above all, they fear for the safety of their children. As we all do."

Thatcher listened in silence. Miles's exemplary self-control slipped a notch.

"But where is this madness going to end?" he demanded suddenly. "I'm almost tempted to believe that Satan has taken a hand at St. Bernadette's. This latest development is—hellish!"

Thatcher knew the word was used literally.

Miles apologized. "But you did not come to hear me recite our troubles. What can I do for you, Mr. Thatcher?"

Carefully, Thatcher told him.

Miles's face closed into an unrevealing mask.

"Francis Omara?" he repeated slowly. "Yes, of course . . ."

He paused. Thatcher remained uncommunicative. This was no time for explanation. Without protracting the moment, Miles went on to provide Thatcher with the description he had requested.

Thatcher nodded to himself, then found alarmingly intelligent eyes fixed upon him.

"I do not want to be premature," he said. "I have the ghost of an idea. Before I can call it more than that, I need more corroboration."

"Yes." Miles sighed painfully. "If only it had been madness."

"Unfortunately," said Thatcher levelly, "greed is far more common."

He left behind him a deeply troubled man. Bankers are not the only realists about human weakness.

Uneasily Miles rose and went to the window. He was in time to see his departing guest emerge in the courtyard below. As he watched, the great snake of Flensburg parents rounded the corner once more to flow past the gates of the Chancery.

Miles narrowed his eyes. Thatcher had stepped forward and hailed one of the marchers. Soon the two were deep in conversation, a pace away from the others.

Miles studied the figure. Was it someone known to him?

Thatcher's companion made a half-turn.

Miles caught his breath.

The face was very familiar indeed.

Thatcher himself finally returned to the Sloan after five o'clock. Many questions had been answered. He knew who had murdered Francis Omara—and why. Only one problem remained. Where was the proof?

He discovered it on Miss Corsa's desk.

She had already left for the day but her neat notes waited him. In many respects they confirmed the obvious. But Miss Corsa, not for the first time, had exceeded her instructions. She had not been content to telephone Kathleen Omara. She had journeyed all the way out to Flensburg. As a result, on her desk were two personal checks, made out to different payees.

Both were signed—Francis P. Omara.

Thatcher studied them sadly. Then he reached for the phone.

23

HEAR INSTRUCTION, AND BE WISE

"All I know is that Mary Foster killed Frank Omara," said Sal Ianello. "And I think I've earned the right to know more."

Sal's eyes were as dark and bright as ever. But days of nonstop negotiation had left his face drawn and his body gaunt. Every now and then he was racked by convulsive, jaw-splitting yawns.

"I am perfectly willing to tell you everything I know,"

John Thatcher replied. "But wouldn't it be better if we let it wait until after you've had some sleep?"

"Now!" said Sal unceremoniously. He was not wasting his last dregs of energy on long sentences. "Why don't you both come for coffee and brandy at our place? We're only two blocks away."

Pat Ianello's instincts as a hostess were activated. She was almost as tired as her husband. "Shouldn't we ask Mr. Ericson too? Just to show there are no hard feelings?"

"I tried," Sal replied. "I don't think I'm his favorite person right now."

"Then let's go."

Thatcher, Dick Unger, and the Ianellos were emerging from the parish hall of St. Bernadette's. There, the Parents League had enthusiastically ratified the agreement reached after days of locked room caucusing. They were all jubilant. St. Bernadette's school would continue. The Unger apartment house would soon begin to rise. And the Sloan was putting up the money. No one was getting what he had originally bargained for. Everyone was beginning to suspect he might be doing even better.

Even Thatcher was slightly exhilarated. He had closed the proceedings with a promise of increased financing. The Parents League had cheered. On his way out, total strangers had pounded him on the back and congratulated him. Even his old neighbor, Harry of the folded arms, had wrung his hand warmly.

It was six days after Mary Foster's arrest. Her confession produced the consensus that had been lacking. The Archdiocese, the Parents League, the police, and even Unger Realty were all eager to heal the festering wound created by the decision to sell St. Bernadette's.

Negotiations had begun immediately. Any tendency to flag had been countered by directives from Rome, City Hall, or the Real Estate Board. The powers-that-be demanded a solution. They got one. Simultaneously a curtain of silence dropped about Mary Foster. The press tried, but lost heart after discovering that all sources of information were locked into a conference room at the Municipal Arbitration Center. On a twenty-four-hour-a-day basis.

This left John Thatcher substituting for Walter Cronkite. Pat Ianello produced a tray with coffee cups and, while Sal circulated with the bottle, put the first question.

"Is it true that Mary was arrested in the church?" She was incredulous. "I thought you couldn't do that."

Thatcher accepted the sugar bowl. "No, not in the church. She was at the rectory. What's more, she had left a message for the police, telling them she was there waiting for them."

This was all news to Sal. "You mean, she knew they were coming for her? How did that happen?"

"Because I talked with Monsignor Miles in the Chancery just before I talked to you on Madison Avenue. I tried to keep my questions as neutral as possible. Nevertheless, he guessed what the result of that line of inquiry would be. By the time I had confirmed my suspicions sufficiently to call the police, he had already conferred with Father Doyle. Father Doyle, of course, reached Mrs. Foster when she returned from picketing. They went to the church together, then they waited for the police at the rectory. It can't have been easy for Father Doyle." Thatcher was remembering the priest's eulogy at Francis Omara's funeral. First there had been the tragedy of burying a man he had seen grow up. Then the heartbreak of hearing confession from a murderer, another parishioner.

Pat Ianello shook her head. "That's what a priest is for, Mr. Thatcher. Father Doyle knows that."

Perhaps fortunately, her husband did not want to spend time on generalities. "Naturally he had to hear Mary's confession. But why did she do it? That's what I want to know."

Thatcher returned to things he understood. "Francis Omara almost told us, in so many words. He said that someone was planning to make money out of the closing of a parochial school."

"I haven't forgotten that. In fact, I thought I knew what he meant when Willard Ericson started his tenants crusade." Sal Ianello had the grace to look apologetic. "Right now, I'd hate to tell you what I figured from that."

"You were not alone, by any means. The police were thinking along the same lines," Thatcher reassured him.

Sal brightened. "They didn't tell me that."

"They told me. They realized that a series of incidents like the one in UN Plaza would encourage absentee landlords to sell out at distress prices. That made them wonder if Omara had been killed to expedite the tenants' crusade. Even while they were explaining their theory, I was bothered by the timing. If the police were right, Francis Omara had smelled a rat long before anything concrete happened. Then, too, publicity about UN Plaza was out of proportion to what might have been expected. Bob Horvath's landlord could have lived someplace else. The Arab and Israeli pickets could have reacted differently. There could have been another human interest story that week which would have drowned the Flensburg effort. There were too many accidents. And without the publicity, the Sirius Meeks protest wouldn't have encouraged a stampede of selling. Then"—Thatcher leaned forward accusingly—"as I was reviewing these objections, I remembered something you told me."

"Something I told you?" Sal Ianello did not believe it.

"Yes. You told me that Mr. Kavanaugh had turned down an offer for his store. And what's more, you told me so the night Ericson launched his campaign. Obviously, somebody was already active in real estate on Jackson Boulevard."

Dick Unger put down his coffee cup and became alert. "Now that is what I want to hear about."

"I shouldn't have to tell you," Thatcher said severely. "After all, from the very start you have been explaining that the new apartment house would raise property values. And this was true until the Parents League went to court and seemed ready for an extended fight. Then, owners of small shops and empty store-fronts could foresee a wait of two or three years before the appreciation materialized. Many of them couldn't wait that long. They'd sell out now, for whatever they could get."

Pat Ianello was seeing the past in her cup. "Mary told me we couldn't hope to create more than a two-year delay. She said that would be enough for her purposes."

"Exactly. She told everybody that. Then, when the owners were sufficiently pessimistic, she bought two buildings—a total of six stores and some overhead apartments—and she was trying for Kavanaugh's store. Once she acquired the real estate she wanted, she probably planned to dishearten the Parents League. She would publicly see the dangers of splitting the parish, she would have second thoughts about opposing the Cardinal, she would see the futility of continued resistance. Then the apartment house would go up, and she would make a very pretty penny."

Dick Unger was engaged in some expert calculations. "She sure would! Do you have any idea how much capital she had?"

"Twenty-two thousand!" Thatcher rapped out.

"Then with the right mortgages . . . my God!" Unger whistled softly. "She would have cleared seventy to eighty thousand. With luck, maybe a hundred thousand. That's nice work, if you can get it."

Sal and Pat were not interested in hypothetical profits. "But how did Frank find out?" Sal asked. "I suppose that's why Mary killed him."

"I think I know what roused his suspicions first." Thatcher reached into his pocket and produced two photostats. "These are the checks for the last two months' rent for your Parents League headquarters. The police have the originals now."

Dick Unger joined the Ianellos at the coffee table. "February first, he paid the rent to Cedar Realty. March first, he paid the rent to Indian Head Realty. Sure. So he knew that the building had been sold." Unger nodded sagely. "And I suppose, if he spent time at the headquarters, he'd gossip with the adjoining storekeepers.

"The police have already discovered that Omara talked with the florist and the baker. Both of them were now paying their rent to Indian Head Realty. Remember, Omara was a businessman. His next step was to find out who owned Indian Head. He did that just before the meeting we all attended. That's why he was so upset. He had realized that—"

Thatcher broke off as Sal Ianello dramatically slapped himself on the forehead.

"Jesus Christ!" Sal exclaimed. "That's why Mary offered to pick up the rent tab for headquarters!"

Pat's eyes sparked. "And she made us think it was generosity! She was afraid we would find out what Frank had."

"Mrs. Foster is a very unscrupulous woman." Thatcher comprehended the Ianellos' anger. No one enjoys recognizing that he has been manipulated. "Francis Omara, on the contrary, was willing to give her every chance. They were the same age, approximately. They had known each other all their lives."

"They were at St. Bernadette's together," Pat reminded herself mournfully.

"And they had worked together at the Parents League. He could not bring himself to accuse her publicly without giving her a chance to justify herself. She used that chance to kill him."

There was silence for several moments. Sal Ianello stumbled to his feet and started to refill glasses. For the first time he noticed two unused cups on the tray. He was grateful for the opportunity to talk about something else.

"Who else is coming?"

His wife answered automatically. "Oh, I asked Bob and Ruthie to drop by if they can manage a sitter." Then she gave a shiver of distaste and straightened pugnaciously. "I'm glad she's been caught. It's so unfair. Someone like Frank killed because Mary wanted an easy way to make money!"

"Well, things stopped being easy for Mrs. Foster thereafter," Thatcher propitiated her. "Having killed Omara because of her property speculation, she wanted to keep everyone's attention riveted on nonprofit aspects of St. Bernadette's. The fates conspired against her. The first thing that happened was the descent of Mrs. Kirk, urging the broad-community viewpoint. Then Unger here wanted you all to come and look at a development he had completed. Mrs. Foster objected to that, I understand?"

"And how!" said a more relaxed Pat.

"But that didn't stop you and your husband from going and from seeing with your own eyes the reclamation of buildings like those on Jackson Boulevard."

Sal was startled. "God! I should have noticed that myself."

"You would have," said Dick Unger, reverting to an old grievance, "if you hadn't been so fixated on that supermarket."

Thatcher leaped into the breach. "But that was nothing compared to Willard Ericson's pyrotechnics. Before she had time to think, he organized a tenants' protest. And after the wild success at UN Plaza, he and Bob Horvath proclaimed that they were going to strip the anonymity from every absentee landlord. Mrs. Foster is far from being a fool. She realized that it was only a matter of time before Indian Head Realty became a target. She had to stop that crusade in its tracks. And, to give her her due, she conceived a remarkably effective plan."

Dick Unger ground his teeth. "By a bomb scare at Unger Realty!"

"A good deal more than that," Thatcher rejoined frostily. "First she disrupted the Sloan Guaranty Trust. Then Unger Realty and the Chancery. All of these were devices to give her time. Her goal, all along, was the Parents League and its direction. For that, she needed more than a scare. So she produced a real bomb at St. Bernadette's School. You know yourself how successful she was. Within two hours she had ousted Ericson from his position of leadership, destroyed even the memory of absentee landlords, and had everybody fully occupied in guarding the school and marching on St. Patrick's."

"She got a lot of help from me." Sal was gloomier than ever.

Pat reached over to squeeze his shoulder. "Never mind, Sal. With Mary on the rampage, you did the right thing. She was probably capable of blowing up the first grade if you hadn't organized everybody."

"The very fact that she didn't had the police focusing on prominent members of the Parents League. They realized that the bomber had arranged things to do as little damage as consonant with his objectives."

Unger weighed this. He always revived when police suspicions pointed in some other direction. "You mean, because the bomb was set for night, when school wasn't in session?"

"More than that." Meticulously Thatcher ticked off his points. "First, the hour chosen was safe. Then, the bomb was arranged in the annex, where damage wouldn't affect operation of the school. It opened us usual, you know, the next morning. Third, the fuse was short enough so that the gas concentration would be minimal. I might add that use of the kitchenette stove suggested a woman. A man could have known about it and planned to use it. But it was certain that all the mothers—who took turns at lunch hour—would think of it instinctively if they were plotting an explosion. On top of that, a beano party was perfect cover for presence in the area. Mrs. Foster simply slipped out for one game, arranged her materials, lit the fuse, and was back inside at her table when the blast came."

Pat Ianello proved that she was not blind to the implications of this statement. "Everything you've said points to a woman, a member of St. Bernadette's, and probably a member of the Parents League. But I fit those qualifications. How did you decide it was Mary Foster?"

"By the property records," Sal answered her. "You don't own Indian Head Realty. Worse luck!"

"The property records were confirmation," Thatcher added quietly. "By the time I talked with Monsignor Miles and with you, I knew who the owner of Indian Head would be."

"All right," Sal offered cheerfully. "I'll be the mug. What did we tell you?"

"Monsignor Miles told me about his last conversation with Francis Omara. Omara had said that it was a terrible thing for one person to use another because it debased them both. He was very troubled."

Unger saw a flaw. "What's new about that? He'd told all of us at the meeting that someone was using the Parents League."

"You've missed the difference. When talking with Miles, he was emphasizing personal relationships. He was upset because *he* had been used."

"I see that," Sal said happily. "But why is it any different? And what did *I* tell you?"

"You repeated what you told me earlier. That the Parents League was really started by Mary Foster, that she persuaded Frank Omara to lead it. I don't think you've grasped the extent of her duplicity. She didn't simply pervert the League. She organized it solely to make a profit. And she used

Omara from the very beginning. That is why everybody is so anxious to clean this up without undue publicity. Neither the Church nor anyone else is happy about the origin of the Parents League."

Sal Ianello certainly was not. His mumblings indicated a revised opinion of Mary Foster.

"Monsignor Miles must have been pretty quick to see what you were getting at," Pat admired. "I would never have known enough to call Father Doyle."

"He's very sensitive to the kind of distinction that Omara was making. Also he recognized one of the basic constraints on the motive for murdering Francis Omara. You just said that you met some of the qualifications for the bomber, Mrs. Ianello. But remember, speculating in property values isn't a crime. Monsignor Miles made that point himself, when he was defending Unger from what he thought were accusations of commercialism. If you made eighty thousand dollars in a way that Flensburg didn't like, there's no reason why it should bother you. You told me yourself that you'll probably move in another year or two. But Mary Foster was a different kettle of fish. She was an ambitious woman with a political future. I suspect that the money was going to fuel that future. She was tied to Flensburg and Flensburg's opinion of her if she was going to run for bigger and better elective offices. She had no other outlets for happiness. And, last but not least, she had just inherited her mother's house. That's where the twenty-two-thousand-dollars capital came from. She sold it two months ago."

Sal Ianello was not rising at the A&P for nothing. "I suppose Monsignor Miles has all sorts of contacts. He could find out all about Mary from political headquarters in Queens."

Thatcher debated the advisability of telling Ianello that the Monsignor had supermarket contacts as well. Then he decided that Ianello had probably already guessed.

"Monsignor Miles had another clue as well. The night he spoke with Omara, Mary Foster was there. At that time, the master list for the League questionnaires was in Omara's possession. Mary claimed that she distributed literature on the night of the murder and then went home. But later on, she had the master list at her house. Of course, she had returned to the storefront and gotten the list before Omara challenged her with his knowledge. After murdering him, she forgot to return the list."

Pat sighed dispiritedly. "It's a nasty story. I can understand why everyone wants to hush it up. But how can they? Won't it all come out at the trial?"

Thatcher was able to answer. "No. Mrs. Foster has agreed to plead guilty to a charge of second-degree murder. She is no more anxious to broadcast the story than anyone else. Her plea is based on the contention that she never premeditated murder. She was simply unnerved by Omara's sudden accusation and lost her head."

"Humph!" snorted the Ianellos in unison.

Further reaction was unnecessary. A good deal of heavy clumping on the stairs plus the resonant echo of a loud voice indicated the arrival of the Horvaths. They swept in, accepted refreshments and apologized for being late.

"It took me longer than I thought to get the kids settled in," Ruthie explained.

"There isn't all that much room in the apartment, but we'll manage," Bob added.

Unger and Thatcher showed their confusion.

"We've taken in Mary Foster's children," Ruthie explained. "Until Larry gets settled."

Bob's laugh rattled glasses. "Come on, Ruthie! Who're you trying to kid?" he scoffed. "Larry Foster'll take damn good care not to get settled until the last one is married."

Ruthie made no attempt to deny this. Instead she said, "Father Doyle says none of this would ever have happened if Larry had been a different kind of man."

Bob stretched comfortably. "He's always been a no-good. I don't mind taking the kids. But I had to miss the meeting. What did you all decide?"

Sal waved a hand at Dick Unger. "He's the expert. He'll tell you."

Obediently, Dick explained. Instead of a twenty-floor apartment building, the new building would have twenty-two floors. The first two stories would house the new St. Bernadette's Parochial School. The school would be maintained

nd provided with utilities by the building management—
Jnger Realty.

Bob Horvath blinked. He opened his mouth and shut it.
Then he spoke: "Now, I'm not an expert or anything. And it
ounds great from our point of view. But who's going to
ent an apartment on top of a school? Christ, the whole point
f schools is to get the kids out of your hair."

Dick Unger warmed to a fellow believer. "That's what I
aid. Believe me, I did! This wasn't my idea." He glared at
al Ianello.

Horvath was still at sea. "But you had to agree to it, didn't
ou?"

Sal and Pat laughed.

Unger could not keep from rubbing the sore. "For five
lays we didn't get anywhere. Then Ianello here has a brain
vave. Does he tell me? Does he tell the Monsignor? Hell,
o!"

Horvath might have been following a serial. "Who did he
ell?"

The explosion came. "He called up my dad. The two of
hem put this deal together over the long-distance line! Dad
ays I don't understand modern parents. They're afraid their
ids will get wet walking to school in the rain. He says we
an raise the price of the apartments!"

"You've got to be kidding." Bob Horvath did not pretend
o understand.

John Thatcher smiled at this forerunner of coming con-
rontation. He raised his glass.

"To the new tenants over St. Bernadette's!" he proposed.
I look forward to seeing what they and Flensburg make of
ach other."